TOO FAST AND TWO DEAD

"Stop!"

Clint's steely voice stopped the man cold. His hand was inches from his dead partner's six-shooter. Clint held his piece steady on the man. Out of the corner of his eye he saw a man wearing a badge approaching.

"Here comes the law," Clint said. "Now, where is Arnie Pace headed?"

"North. Just north, I swear!"

"What's going on here?" the sheriff shouted. He had his hand on his gun and looked ready to use it.

"Sheriff," Clint said, turning to face him, "my name is Clint Adams and I—"

At that moment Roberts saw his only chance. He grabbed his partner's gun and yanked it from the holster. Clint heard the sound of metal on leather, turned and fired once. The bullet hit Roberts in the chest, and exploded in his heart. He fell dead.

"Mister," the sheriff said, looking at the two bodies, "you got one *helluva* lot of explainin' to do."

DON'T MISS THESE ALL-ACTION WESTERN SERIES FROM THE BERKLEY PUBLISHING GROUP

THE GUNSMITH by J. R. Roberts

Clint Adams was a legend among lawmen, outlaws, and ladies. They called him . . . the Gunsmith.

LONGARM by Tabor Evans

The popular long-running series about U.S. Deputy Marshal Long—his life, his loves, his fight for justice.

SLOCUM by Jake Logan

Today's longest-running action Western. John Slocum rides a deadly trail of hot blood and cold steel.

BUSHWHACKERS by B. J. Lanagan

An action-packed series by the creators of Longarm! The rousing adventures of the most brutal gang of cutthroats ever assembled—Quantrill's Raiders.

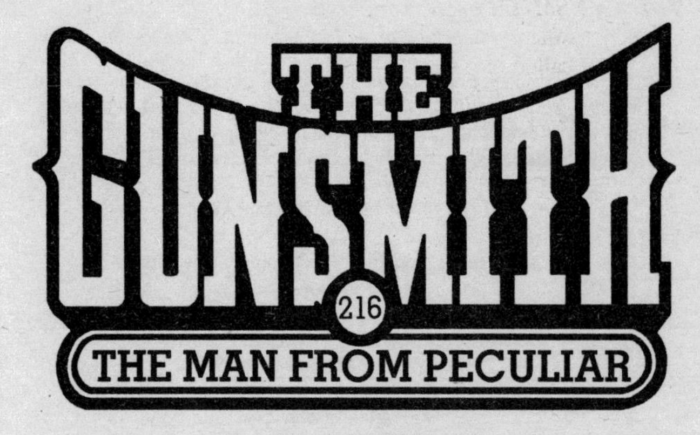

J. R. ROBERTS

JOVE BOOKS, NEW YORK

This is a work of fiction. Names, characters, places, and incidents are either the product of the author's imagination or are used fictitiously, and any resemblance to actual persons, living or dead, business establishments, events, or locales is entirely coincidental.

THE MAN FROM PECULIAR

A Jove Book / published by arrangement with
the author

PRINTING HISTORY
Jove edition / December 1999

For information address: The Berkley Publishing Group,
a division of Penguin Putnam Inc.,
375 Hudson Street, New York, New York 10014.

The Penguin Putnam Inc. World Wide Web site address is
http://www.penguinputnam.com

ISBN: 0-515-12708-6

A JOVE BOOK®
Jove Books are published by The Berkley Publishing Group,
a division of Penguin Putnam Inc.,
375 Hudson Street, New York, New York 10014.
JOVE and the "J" design
are trademarks belonging to Penguin Putnam Inc.

PRINTED IN THE UNITED STATES OF AMERICA

10 9 8 7 6 5 4 3 2 1

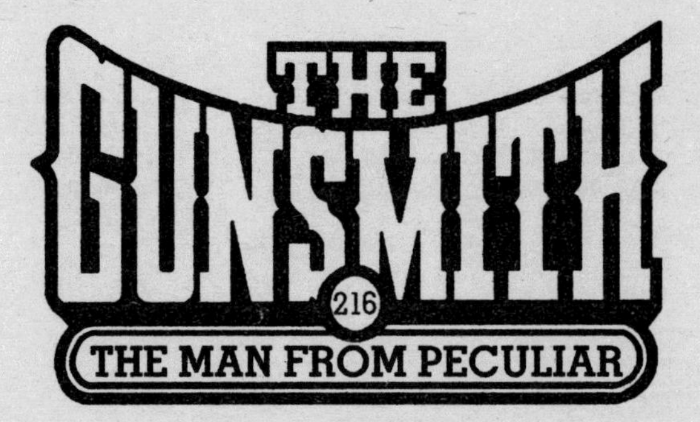
THE
GUNSMITH
216
THE MAN FROM PECULIAR

PROLOGUE

He had given his life to God, and God had forsaken him. Why else would his wife and young son be lying in their graves well before their time, victims of as violent a death as could have been visited upon them?

"Reverend?"

He turned to look at another well wisher, another of Peculiar, Missouri's, citizens who had come to pay their respects.

"Mrs. Ford," he said.

"My mister and me, we're so sorry."

"I know," Reverend Land said. "God bless you for coming."

"Someone should hunt those animals down and put them in *their* graves for what they done . . . if you'll forgive me for sayin' so."

Land took the middle-aged housewife's hands in his and said, "God will forgive you, I'm sure, Mrs. Ford."

"Thank you, Reverend," she said, with tears in her eyes, "and God bless you."

He smiled and nodded even though he wanted to say, God has forsaken me. There could be no other explanation for what had happened.

He had been in town, at the church, preparing for a

bazaar that was to be held just days from now, when five men on horseback had ridden up to his house outside of town. Knowing his wife, he knew she must have offered them refreshments, but in minutes she had been raped and murdered, and their seven-year-old son had been shot in the head—perhaps when the brave little lad had gone to his mother's aid.

The five had been spotted before and after the incident, by two different people who placed them near the scene of the tragedy. Combining the two reports the Reverend John David Land had a pretty good idea what they looked like.

He fended off the good wishes of other parishioners, until it was just he and Sheriff Andy Worth standing there. The two men had been friends for most of the ten years that Reverend Land had been in Peculiar.

"What now, John David?" Worth asked. "Continue God's work?"

Land looked at Worth and the expression on his face was so benign that his words shocked the lawman.

"Continue preaching the word of a murderer? Not likely, Andy."

"John David!" Worth said, looking around quickly to see if anyone else had heard the blasphemy from the Reverend's mouth. "I can understand your anger, but you're a man of God—" He stopped himself before he could say, "For Chrissake!"

"Was, Andy," Land said, "was. I was something else before I was called by God, and it looks like I'll have to go back to that."

"And what was that, John David?"

Land opened his mouth to reply, then thought better of it. Instead, he simply said, "A man, Andy . . . just a man."

He turned and walked away from the graves, watched by the man who had known him for ten years, who was thinking at that moment that maybe he didn't know John David Land all that well at all.

John David Land went to the church for the last time. The thing he needed most was there. Luckily, it had not been in the house which had served as a funeral pyre for everything else he held dear, or owned. No, this item was in the church, in his office, under lock and key, and he had not held it or beheld it in many years.

He went to the trunk in his office, unlocked it and tossed the key aside. He would not be needing it ever again. He reached into the trunk and removed the black shirt and jeans and the gun and holster that were wrapped in cloth. As he removed the cloth, the metal of the gun gleamed. He touched it, the way a man touches an old lover he has come upon again, not because he loved it so much as because it would be the instrument of his vengeance.

When he'd come to peculiar and married Miriam he had promised her that he would never again wear a gun. He must have known though, deep down, that he would need it again, so he had never gotten rid of it.

He undressed and slowly donned the dark clothing, which he had not worn for as long as he had put down his gun. It fit a little tight—Miriam had fed him well over the years—but it would do.

Next he picked up the holster, spread it and strapped it to his waist. He stood there a moment, feeling the weight on his hips and was surprised to find that it was as if it had never left him.

He'd fired a gun only once in the past ten years, and that was at a turkey shoot, where he'd won a turkey for a family who could not afford the entry fee to compete. He'd assured everyone at the time that it had been a lucky shot, directed more by God's aim than his own.

Now he palmed the gun, not clumsily as one might have expected, but smoothly and with ease. Apparently, this was something that, once learned, was never forgotten.

The gun nestled in his hand like an old friend, and just for that moment he wondered why he had ever put it down. But he knew why. God had sent him Miriam, and had then called him. If he had known, however, what was to come in the future, he never would have answered that call. If he hadn't—and if he hadn't been away, tending to others while his own family was being killed—perhaps they'd be alive today.

He holstered the gun and, looking up, held his last conversation with God.

"If this is a test, Oh Lord, I reckon I've failed. But then, so have you."

ONE

One month earlier . . .

Peculiar was a peculiar name for a town.

Clint Adams had been to many towns in Missouri, and being in Missouri reminded him of his friendship with Frank and Jesse James. He wondered, however, if even Frank and Jesse had ever been to Peculiar.

So Clint rode into Peculiar, mostly to soothe his curiosity than for any real need to stop somewhere. At first glance, however, the town looked like any other town, with a couple of hotels, a couple of saloons, a general store, a feed and grain, a hardware store—all the businesses you'd expect to see on the main street of any town. Whatever made Peculiar peculiar was not immediately evident.

He finally decided to rein in Duke in front of one of the saloons and get himself a drink. If anyone would know how the town got its name, a bartender would.

He entered the saloon and wasn't surprised to find it empty that early in the day. He went up to the bar where the bartender smiled at him like he was the first customer of the day.

"What can I get ya?"

"Beer."

"Comin' up."

"A little early for most people?" Clint asked.

"That's the way we are around here," the man said, setting a full mug down in front of him. "Nobody really starts drinkin' until after three—and that includes the town drunk."

"That's kind of peculiar," Clint said, and from the look on the bartender's face it wasn't the first time he'd heard some sort of joke like that.

"Okay, sorry," Clint said.

"That's okay," the man said. "It is a pretty odd name for a town."

"How did it get that name, anyway?"

The bartender leaned his elbows on the bar and said, "You know, nobody seems to know for sure. There are a couple of stories."

"Which one do you believe?"

"None of them," the barman said, "I'm holding out for something real interesting."

"Well, what's one of the uninteresting ones?"

"Settler came from the east, all following one man who said he had a 'vision.' When they reached this place the man said how it was peculiar, but this looked just like the spot he'd seen in his vision. So, they built the town, and called it Peculiar."

"You're right," Clint said, "it needs a better story."

"You passin' through?"

"That's right," Clint said. "Curiosity more than anything else brought me to town. Tell me, how come nobody drinks before three?"

"Our reverend frowns on it."

"Oh? A God-fearing town, is it?"

The barman scratched his grey stubble and said, "I ain't never figured out if they fear God, or the Reverend."

"I see. What about you?"

"Don't put much stock in religion, myself. You?"

"Haven't given it much thought, lately," Clint admitted, "but I have known some preachers I've liked. What kind of fellow is yours?"

"Nice enough," the bartender said. "Ain't never heard none of his sermons, myself, so I can't say how he is behind the pulpit."

Just for want of something to talk about, Clint continued the conversation about the preacher.

"How old a man is he?"

"Oh, well, I guess he's about thirty-five or six."

"Got yourself one of the young ones. Does he have a family?"

"Sure does. Pretty wife and a young'n—boy, about seven or so."

"So I guess he's a pretty happy man."

"You'd think so, but whenever I see him on the street he's always frownin'. Never looks all that happy to me."

"Must have a lot on his mind," Clint said, "you know, fighting the good fight and all."

"Once or twice I said to him, 'morning Reverend Land', but I soon got tired of bein' ignored."

"Maybe it's because you run a saloon?"

"Could be."

"Land," Clint said, almost as an afterthought, "Land . . . that's not a common name. Where have I heard it?"

"Can't say," the bartender replied. "Don't think you heard of this feller. Nobody hears nothin' that happens here in Peculiar."

"Land," Clint said again, tasting it, turning it over. The name was very familiar, and this would bother him until he brought it to the surface.

"This preacher, would he be at the church now?"

"More'n likely. Either there or his house."

"And where's that?"

"Just outside of town a few miles. You just keep

goin' the way you was goin' and you can't miss it. Why you so interested?''

''The name is not common,'' Clint said, again, ''and I think I knew somebody by that name, once.''

''A friend?''

''No.''

''A preacher?''

''Not that, either.''

''Guess that gnaws at ya, when you think somethin' is familiar to you and you can't think of it.''

''That's why I think if I see him, maybe it'll jog my memory.''

''Well, like I said,'' the man remarked, ''either the church or his house.''

Clint paid for the beer and said, ''Much obliged. Hope it gets busier for you.''

''Don't worry,'' the bartender said, ''it will.''

Clint walked around Peculiar and located the church. He went inside, but it was empty. During the walk he remembered the name Land, and what it had been associated with. It didn't seem that the Land he was thinking of would have ended up as a preacher, but stranger things had happened.

He left the church and wondered if he should mount up and ride out to the preacher's house. What would he tell the man and his family? That he was wondering if *this* Land was the Land he remembered from . . . when? Eight, ten years ago?

Clint decided to take Duke to the livery and then get himself a hotel room. He was in no hurry to get anywhere. He could afford to spend a day or two to sastisfy his idle curiosity. Besides, Peculiar seemed like a nice, quiet little town, and he could use a day or two of peace and quiet.

TWO

Arnie Pace sat his horse quietly and studied the farm at the bottom of the rise.

"So whatta we do, Pace?" Jim Smith asked. Pace always called him "Jimmy Boy."

Pace didn't reply. Paxton Lewis nudged the twenty-year-old Jimmy Boy into silence. "I'm thinkin'."

Bruce Roberts nudged Ted Lowell, and both laughed under their breath.

Pace continued to study the situation down below for a good fifteen minutes or so, long enough for the horses to get edgy and start to fidget.

Finally, he said, "No."

"No? Why not?" Jimmy Boy demanded.

Pace hardly turned his body and the back of his hand knocked Jimmy Boy off his horse. The boy landed on his back so hard all the air was knocked out of him. He laid there making gasping noises, feeling like he was going to die until finally he was able to take a breath.

"Jeez—" he gasped.

"You want to ride down there be my guest, Jimmy Boy," Pace said, "but that farmer carries a rifle with him even when he goes to the outhouse, and my bet is he knows how to use it. Sure, we'd take him, but at least one of us would take a bullet before it was all over. You want that to be you?''

Jimmy Boy opened his mouth, but didn't have enough breath yet to answer.

''He didn't mean nothin' by it, Pace,'' Pax Lewis said.

''He's your kin, Pax,'' Mace said, ''that's the only reason he's here. Don't make me regret the decision.''

''You won't, Pace.''

''Get him up on his horse, then,'' Mace said. ''You two can catch up to us. We're gonna look for easier pickin's.''

He turned his horse and rode away, followed by Lowell and Roberts.

Pax got off his horse and pulled his nephew to his feet.

''What the hell is wrong with you?'' he demanded.

Jimmy Boy coughed and gasped for breath a few seconds more, holding his hand to his chest.

''That farmer . . . didn't look . . . so tough . . . to me,'' he stammered.

''One thing you better get straight, Jimmy Boy,'' Pax Lewis said. ''You're ridin' with the Pace Gang, and that means you follow Pace's orders. Got it?''

''I got it,'' Jimmy Boy said. His eyes were still watering from the blow, and out of shame.

''Good. Get mounted, then. We don't want to get left behind.''

Jimmy Boy picked his hat up off the ground, slapped it against himself to get rid of some of the dust on it and on him, and then mounted up. The farmer hadn't looked so tough. Pace was getting old. He must be damned near forty, his Uncle Paxton's age. What this gang needed was a new leader who was young enough to try some new things—or maybe what Jimmy Boy needed to do was start his own gang.

Yeah, that was it. The Jimmy Smith gang, and he

wouldn't allow anybody in it who was older than, say, twenty-five.

"You comin'?" Pax called, impatiently.

"Yeah," Jimmy Smith said, "I'm comin'," and then added to himself, "for now."

THREE

Clint's room in the Peculiar Hotel was cleaner than most, the bed a welcome change from the hard ground. Clint still didn't think he could settle down in any one place and live, but an occasional stop in a hotel or a friend's home was a welcome change. The closest he could come to having a home was Labyrinth, Texas, where he spent a lot of his time when he wasn't wandering around. Sometimes he'd hit the trail—like now—and just travel aimlessly. This was why he felt he could afford a couple of days in Peculiar to satisfy his curiousity—first about the town itself, and also about this Reverend Land.

He left his saddlebags and rifle in the room and went in search of a meal. His intention had been to ask someone—the desk clerk, the bartender—to recommend a place, but as it turned out he needed only to follow his nose. Someone was doing wonderful things with beef, and he followed the aroma to a small café just around the corner from the hotel.

The place didn't have a name, but a big plate glass window that simply said CAFÉ in big, capital letters. He went inside and found it half full. It was not lunch time, and too early for dinner, so apparently it was simply an eatery that was popular with the locals.

"Help ya?" a waiter asked, wiping his hands on his once-white apron.

Clint looked around before answering, spotted the table he wanted and said, "Yes, could I have that back table, please?"

"Sure," the waiter said. "Follow me."

The waiter seated him and asked him what he wanted.

"I want a pot of strong coffee and whatever it is that's making that delicious smell."

The waiter smiled and said, "That's the cook's special beef stew. He makes it every Wednesday."

"Is that why all these people are here?"

"Yep," the waiter said. "There's a lunch rush and a dinner rush, and these folks are tryin' to beat both—like you."

"Well, bring me a big bowl of it and I'll be a happy man if it tastes as good as it smells."

"It does," the waiter said. "I'll put in your order and bring out your coffee."

"Thanks."

While he waited, Clint surveyed the room for potential trouble. He saw mostly tables of two—three couples eating but not speaking to each other, and four tables of two men sitting together, doing the same. Apparently, the stew was good enough to suspend conversation—and curiosity, for hardly any of the people in the room had looked up when he—a stranger—had entered.

The waiter brought the coffee out and it was as Clint had asked—strong. This spoke well for the possibility of the stew being as good as advertised. Clint had had beef stew in many places, some of it excellent, and he was looking forward to sampling this cook's Wednesday special.

When the waiter finally appeared again, it was with a

steaming, heaping bowl of beef and vegetables, which he placed before Clint with a flourish.

"Cook would like to know what you think when you taste it, and if you don't like it we won't charge you,"

To make a guarantee like that they must have *known* how good it was.

"I'll let you know."

"Enjoy."

And he did. He'd tasted better only a time or two before, and neither of those times was he in a restaurant, which meant that this was almost as good as home-cooked beef stew.

Finding good food in a new town was always a plus.

He paid for his meal, assuring the waiter that it was excellent and well worth paying for.

"Come back again," the waiter said.

"Anyplace else in town got decent food?"

The waiter grinned and said, "You want to take all your meals here."

"Okay, thanks."

"See you again."

"Yeah."

He left the café, rounded the corner and went back to the saloon he had been in earlier in the day. It was starting to fill up as people finished their work days, but there was still plenty of room at the bar.

"Hey, back again," the bartender said. "Did you find the preacher?"

"No, not yet."

"Decided to stay?"

"A day or two," Clint said.

"What can I get ya?"

"A beer."

"Comin' up."

Clint turned to survey the room again, a habit he'd gotten into over the years and one that had served him well. No one seemed to be paying any special attention to him, which suited him fine. In one corner, four men had started a game of five card stud, and there were two open chairs at the table.

"That a regular game?" he asked the bartender as the man set down his beer.

"Oh yeah, they been playin' together a long time."

"What about the empty chairs?"

"They'll probably get filled in another hour or so. You want to play until then? I can get you in."

"No," Clint said, "I try not to play in regular games. Everybody knows everybody."

"They don't cheat," the man assured him.

"Each other," Clint said, "they don't cheat each other. It's been my experience that the stranger at the table is at a disadvantage."

"Suit yourself," the bartender said and went to the other end of the bar to get someone a drink. Clint hoped the man wasn't offended, but he wasn't about to go against one of his rules just to keep from offending a bartender.

The bartender came back, apparently not offended.

"So what happened that you didn't see the reverend?" he asked.

"I went to the church but he wasn't there. I was too tired to ride out to his house. Maybe I'll catch him at his place of business tomorrow."

The bartender chuckled and said, " 'Place of business.' I like that."

"Does he ever come in here?"

"Never," the man said. "If the Reverend does any drinkin', he does it someplace else."

"Another saloon?"

"Nope," the bartender said. "Either church or home."

"Or not at all."

"I hope not."

"Why?"

"I don't trust a man who don't even take a drink once in a while."

Everybody had his own philosophy, Clint decided. That was as good as any he'd heard.

"Sure about that game?" the man asked.

"Positive."

"I got work to do. Holler when you want another one. On the house."

"I'll be hollering," Clint assured him.

FOUR

Reverend John David Land sat across the table from his wife, the wonderful dinner she had cooked spread out before them. To his right sat their seven-year-old son, Joshua. But neither the Reverend nor his wife, Miriam, were paying special attention to the meal.

"Don't you want to talk about it?" she asked him.

"Talk about what?"

"Whatever it is that's bothering you. You never come home from your church early."

"There's nothing wrong," he assured her. "I just wanted to spend some time with my family."

Miriam was quick enough to grab Joshua's glass when the boy knocked it over with his arm. He was a smaller, clumsier version of his father, who already had some food on the sleeve of his jacket.

"Drink your milk," she said, righting the glass without spilling a drop, "don't spread it around."

"Yes, Mommy."

Land stared across the table at his wife, loving her more than he ever had before. How could he tell her that the past had come riding into Peculiar and come looking for him?

He didn't know Clint Adams, had never met the man

but, of course, he knew of his reputation. When he received word that Adams was looking for him, he left the church and went home. He didn't know if he could avoid the matter totally but was hoping that the next morning the man would simply leave town.

Neither was he afraid of Clint Adams. Actually, it might have done him some good to see the man he could have become had he not found God. However, he didn't want to take any chances with his happiness, though, or the happiness of his family.

Why Adams was looking for him he didn't know. As far as he knew he'd never even crossed paths with the man.

"You're so far away," Miriam said, reaching out for his hand. "Can't you tell me what it is?"

"It's nothing, Miriam," he said. "Nothing. Let's eat this wonderful dinner you've prepared."

As far as Miriam Land knew, her husband had never before lied to her. Perhaps he thought he wasn't lying to her now. Maybe he thought he was sparing her—but from what?

She sighed and picked up the bowl of potatoes, put some in her plate and passed it on. She trusted that he would tell her in his own good time.

After dinner, Land went outside on the porch to smoke his pipe. Miriam didn't like when he smoked it in the house. He lit it, sucked until it was burning to his satisfaction, then extinguished the match and tossed it into the dirt.

What could he tell Miriam that would put her mind to rest and yet not be the truth? Because if he told her the truth, if he told her about the life he'd once led, what would she do then? She'd had a sheltered upbringing and wouldn't understand a man like Clint Adams.

It was not a chance he was willing to take.

FIVE

Clint resisted the lure of the only poker game in the saloon. It was something he enjoyed, something he occasionally used to fill the time, but he stood by his rule of never joining a regular game.

He had another beer and tried to bring up from the depths of his memory why the name "Land" struck a chord with him. He must have met someone by that name, or crossed paths with him, or read something about him.

And then he had it.

"That's it," he said, slamming the palm of his hand down on the bar loud enough to attract attention.

"Need somethin'?" the bartender appeared to ask.

"Yes," Clint said, "a better memory."

"Don't think I can do anything about that," the bartender said. "How about another beer, though?"

"I don't think so," Clint said. He decided not to confide to the man the return of his memory concerning the name "Land"—at least, not until he found out whether or not he was right.

"I'm turning in," he said. "Good night."

"G'night," the bartender said. "Come on back tomorrow."

"I will," Clint said, "if I'm still in town."

He was on his way to the door when a man stepped into the saloon, wearing a badge. He also wore a well-worn gun and holster which looked as if they had seen a lot of use. He looked around the room, locked his eyes on Clint and came walking over.

"Evenin', Sheriff," the bartender said. "A beer?"

"Only if Mr. Adams here will have one with me," Sheriff Andy Worth said.

"I was just leaving . . . ."

"Oh, just stay long enough to have another beer with me," Worth said. "I want to talk to you about somethin'."

Clint hesitated just a moment, then said, "All right, one more beer."

Clint and the sheriff took their drinks to a back table.

"I expect you'll want to sit with your back to the wall," the sheriff said. "Your kind usually do."

"My kind?" Clint repeated, but he did indeed take the chair with his back to the wall.

"The kind that live by the gun," the sherriff said, sitting opposite him.

"I see you wear a gun, Sheriff."

"It's a tool of my job," the lawman said. "I don't live by it."

"Did you invite me to sit so you could scold me, or insult me about the way I live my life?"

"Neither," the sheriff said, and paused to take a sip of his beer. "This is a nice quiet town, Mr. Adams. I was wondering what you were doing here."

"I'm just passing through."

"And plan to stay how long? Till morning, maybe?"

"I think my horse needs a little more rest than that, Sheriff," Clint said. "I figure a couple of days."

"And how do you figure to spend those days?"

"Quietly," Clint said, "and peacefully."

"Well, that's good to hear," the lawman said.

They sat in silence for a few moments, working on their beers, and Clint decided to leave it to the other man to break it.

"I was just wonderin' . . . ," the sheriff finally said.

"Wondering what, Sheriff?"

"Are you a church-goin' man, Adams?"

"Not particularly."

"That's funny," the man said.

"What is?"

"Well, somebody said they saw you goin' into the church earlier today."

"Somebody's right."

"But you just said you ain't a church-goin' man."

"I don't attend church services, Sheriff," Clint said, "but I like churches, in general. I like the way they feel. I like how quiet and dark they are. Sometimes I just go into a church to relax and get out of the sun."

"Was that your reason for goin' there today?"

It was all the questions about the church that made Clint think that this was the real reason the lawman had come looking for him. It had something to do with the church, and with him looking for the Reverend Land.

"Well, no," Clint said, "it wasn't."

He let the lawman stew.

"Well then, why did you go?" the man finally asked.

"First," Clint said, "before I answer that, I think I'd like to know why you're asking."

"I'm the law here, Adams," the man said. "I do the askin'."

"Well, in that case," Clint said, "I think this conversation is over."

SIX

''It ain't over until I say it's over,'' Sheriff Andy Worth said.

Clint had to admire the man for not backing down.

''You'll have to give a little to get a little, Sheriff.''

''Whataya mean?''

''Why are you asking me all these questions?''

''Because it's my job.''

''There's another reason, isn't there?''

''Like what?''

''Could it have something to do with my visit to the church?''

Worth didn't answer.

''Or the fact that I was looking for your Reverend Land?''

''Why?'' Worth asked, then. ''Why are you looking for the Reverend?''

Clint studied the lawman for a few moments and then said, ''Let me guess. You and he are friends.''

''Real good friends.''

''For how long?''

''As long as he's lived here.''

''Ten years?''

''Nine or ten. Why?''

"The name is familiar to me, that's all," Clint said. "The last name, Land. I was just . . . curious."

"So that's what this is all about?" Worth asked. "Your curiosity?"

"That's it."

Worth sat back.

"I thought maybe you were, uh . . ."

"That I was looking for him to kill him?"

Worth shrugged.

"Why would I do that?"

Another shrug.

"Did he tell you that might be the reason I was looking for him?" Clint asked.

"He didn't tell me much," Worth admitted. "Just that you were here and that you had come to the church."

"What's your Reverend's full name?"

"John David Land," Worth said.

"John David," Clint said, repeating it a couple of times—and then it came to him. J. D. Land!

"Recognize it?"

"Hmm? Oh, no," Clint lied. "No, no. I must have been thinking of someone else."

"Well, all right, then. Your curiosity is satisfied, I guess."

"I guess. Except . . ."

"Except what?"

"I'd like an opportunity to apologize if I caused him any discomfort." Clint said. "Do you think you could arrange for that to happen?"

"I'm sure I can," Worth said, pushing his chair back. "The Reverend Land is a very forgiving man. I'll let you know tomorrow."

As the lawman walked away, Clint thought that the J. D. Land he remembered hearing about wasn't a very forgiving man at all.

SEVEN

"Why does he want to see me?" Reverend Land asked Sheriff Andy Worth.

"He says he wants to apologize."

"Couldn't he apologize through you?"

Worth studied his friend for a moment.

"If you don't want to see him, John David, you don't have to," the lawman said. He was the only person who consistently called the Reverend "John David." The only other person who did it was Miriam, and that was only when she was angry with him—which was not often.

"If you're worried that he's a gunman, I can be there—"

"No, no," Land said, "it's all right, Andy. Would you ask him to come by the church in the morning? I can speak with him then."

"That's fine," Worth said. "Since it's late now, I'll stop by his hotel tomorrow and tell him.

"Okay, thanks."

Worth thought there was something else going on inside his friend's head, but it was obvious he wasn't going to hear what it was. He stepped down off the porch, mounted his horse and headed back to town.

As the sound of his horse's hoofbeats faded, the door to the house opened and Miriam Land came out.

"Did you hear?" her husband asked.

"Yes," she said, "I eavesdropped."

"You didn't have to do that," he told her. "I would have told you everything."

"I know."

She came up next to him, and he put his arm around her waist.

"Is the boy asleep?"

"Yes."

They stood in silence for a while, just looking out into the darkness.

"John, did you know this man Adams?"

"No, but I knew of him."

"What if he recognizes you?"

"He won't," Land said. "We've never met."

"But what if he does, and he wants to . . . challenge you?"

"Miriam," Land said, "this man is reputed to be the fastest, deadliest gun around—and perhaps ever. He has nothing to prove by challenging me to a gunfight. Shooting down a man of God is not going to enhance his reputation."

"Then why was he looking for you in the first place?"

"As Andy said, the name Land struck a chord with him and he was curious. Tomorrow I'll satisfy his curiosity and accept his apology, and he'll be on his way with no harm done."

She tightened her arm around his waist and said, "I hope so."

"Why don't you go inside and get ready for bed?" he said. "I'll be in in a minute or so."

"All right, but don't be long."

He kissed the top of her head and said, "I won't be."

She went back in the house, and he continued to stare

out into the darkness, thinking about his meeting tomorrow with Clint Adams. There was never any telling of how accurate a man's reputation was. He was just going to have to wait until tomorrow morning to find out what kind of man Clint Adams was.

EIGHT

Clint woke up the next morning with a warm, naked hip pressed up against his. He turned his head and saw it wasn't a hip, but a very pleasing buttock cheek. He frowned, taking a moment to remember who the butt cheek belonged to. The long, dark hair that was fanned out over the pillow helped, and he recalled the saloon girl named Randy who had approached him after the sheriff left the saloon.

"You a friend of the sheriff's?"

He looked up at her and saw a very pretty face, pale skin, black hair and a pair of breasts the approximate size and consistancy of ripe peaches.

"I never even met him before," Clint said.

"Just passing through town?"

"I should be here for a couple of days," he said. "What did you have in mind?"

She laughed and said, "Wow, you don't waste time, do you?"

He smiled and said, "You came up to me, remember?"

Now she looked shy.

"All right, you caught me. You look . . . different from everyone else in this town."

"That's because I am," he said. "I guess I'm just not as peculiar as everyone else here."

She laughed and said, "I guess not. Can I get you a beer?"

He'd intended to go back to his hotel when he finished the beer he had, but said. "Sure. Bring me another."

She'd brought him another beer and sat down to talk, and they ended up going back to his room together.

He put his hand on her butt cheek and began to rub it in slow circular movements. She moaned and rolled onto her stomach, giving him a fine view of both cheeks, which he started rubbing. She moaned again, and this time he could tell that she was awake. He slid down and began to kiss her buttocks, running his tongue over them. Her skin was smooth and smelled great, and from between her legs another fragrance rose to tickle his nostrils. He slid his hand beneath her to cup her and found her wet. He got to his knees, then took hold of her hips to raise them up. She obliged by getting to her hands and knees and he entered her that way, sliding his penis up between her thighs. She was slick and hot, and he slid in easily. They began to slap against each other, slowly at first, then more quickly until the sound of flesh slapping flesh filled the room. Moments after that the sound of their grunting joined in, and then they both cried out as they neared the end of their morning wake-up.

"I just love waking up that way," Randy said, lying on her back and watching him get dressed.

"We can try it again tomorrow morning, too, if you like," he told her. "That is, unless I get a better offer."

She laughed and said, "There's no better offer in town, Clint. You were with the best last night."

"Then I guess it's a date for tonight, huh?"

"You better believe it."

Fully dressed, he leaned over her to kiss the nipples of each small, firm breast, and then kissed her hungry mouth. It was a kiss that almost lured him back into bed with her.

"I'll see you later, kid," he said and went out the door.

Randy had already told Clint that she didn't eat breakfast, but he did, and he was starving. Must have been all the exercise he had gotten the night before.

For breakfast he decided to try the hotel dining room. He had ordered steak and eggs but had not gotten them yet when the sheriff came walking in. He spotted Clint and walked over to his table.

"You're not going to ruin my breakfast by telling me to get out of town, are you, Sheriff?"

"No," Worth said. "I just wanted to let you know that the Reverend agreed to see you today."

"Well, good. I'm glad to hear that."

"I offered to be there when you meet, but he turned me down."

"I don't think there's any reason for the law to be present, Sheriff. I'm just going to give the man my apologies."

"See that's all you do, Adams," Worth said. "I mean it. The Reverend has a lot of friends around here."

"I'll bear that in mind, Sheriff."

"See that you do."

"Care to join me for some coffee? Or breakfast?" Clint asked.

"Sorry," Worth said, "maybe another time. I've got some work to do."

"Sure," Clint said, "some other time, then."

The lawman turned and walked away, and the waiter came with Clint's breakfast. He'd been afraid that he wasn't going to be able to eat his steak and eggs. The sheriff seemed to take his job very seriously, and if the Reverend had not agreed to see Clint, he was sure the lawman would have tried to run him out of town.

''Tell me something,'' Clint said to the waiter.

''Sir?''

''Do you know the Reverend Land?''

''Oh, yes, sir.''

''What do you think of him?''

''Well, in my humble opinion,'' said the fiftyish waiter, ''he is the salvation of this town's soul.''

''So,'' Clint said, cutting into his steak, ''I guess that means you like him.''

NINE

There was no reason to think that anyone in Peculiar didn't like the Reverend, and there was also no reason for Clint to keep asking. After all, all he was doing was trying to satisfy his curiosity. If the man was who he thought he was, there really wasn't any reason to let *him* know that Clint knew.

After breakfast, Clint walked over to the church. It was just as empty as it had been the day before, except for one man standing up near the altar. He was tall, slender, dressed all in black. Preachers and gamblers, Clint thought, both had black wardrobes—and it worked for both.

"Reverend?"

Clint saw the man's shoulders hunch, just for a moment, before he said without turning, "Mr. Adams?"

"That's right."

The Reverend turned around. He was no one Clint had ever seen before—but he expected that.

"I understand you've been looking for me," Land said.

Clint moved closer. Reverend Land looked to be in his mid-thirties. That would be about right.

"Yes, I have."

"May I ask why?"

"Just to satisfy my curiosity."

"About what?"

"Your name—Land—it sounded familiar to me."

"Did it?"

"Yes," Clint said. "Have you ever heard of J. D. Land?"

"J. D.," the Reverend said, "those are my initials. John David."

"That's what the sheriff said. You've got a good friend there. He's looking out for you."

"I have a lot of friends in town," Land said. He then looked up and added, "and one very good one out of town."

"Friends are handy things to have."

"So," Land said, "now that you've seen me, and met me, what now?"

"Well, you obviously aren't the J. D. Land that I was looking for," Clint said, "so I guess I'll be on my way . . . except . . ."

"Except what?"

"Well, I promised somebody I'd stay until tomorrow, and I'd hate to break that promise."

"I don't see any reason why you should have to. In fact, why don't you come out to the house later tonight, meet my wife, and have supper with us."

"Well, that's very nice of you, Reverend."

"She's a wonderful cook."

"And I haven't had a home-cooked meal in months."

"Good, then it's settled. Say six o'clock?"

"Six o'clock," Clint repeated. "I'll be there."

Land came down from the altar and extended his hand to Clint. The two men shook, and Clint got an even closer look at Land.

"I'll tell her we're having company," he said. "She loves to cook for people."

"For hungry people, I hope."

"See you then."

As Clint left the church, John David Land thought he had done the right thing. The man didn't seem to recognize him, and bringing him home for a meal would allay any fears that Miriam had.

This hadn't been so bad, after all.

After Clint left the church, he walked slowly back to his hotel. It was too early to stop in a saloon, and he was sure Randy would still be warming his bed.

He'd been surprised when Land had invited him home for a meal. The man must have been dead sure that he hadn't been recognized, but indeed he had. John David Land had, ten years ago, been J. D. Land, a young gunman who people were saying was the next Wild Bill Hickok. He'd already killed several men by the time he was twenty-four and was on his way to bigger and greater things—in some people's eyes—when, one day, he simply vanished. No more newspaper accounts, and soon the "J. D. Land" sightings stopped, much the way the Hickok sightings had. It seemed that some people thought legends *never* died. Not that Clint ever felt he was a legend, but he wondered how many sightings there would be after he was gone?

He quickened his pace, hoping he would catch Randy before she got dressed and left the room.

Sheriff Andy Worth watched from across the street as Clint Adams came out of the church and walked away toward his hotel. He'd been ready to walk into the house of God at the first sign of trouble and was relieved that he hadn't had to. Still, he couldn't help but be curious about how the meeting between the two men went.

After all, when one gunman with a reputation met another, there were usually sparks.

TEN

After spending a strenuous afternoon with Randy, who was, indeed, still in his bed in his hotel room when he got back, Clint left the hotel and walked over to the saloon. There were only a few patrons in the place, as it was still too early in the day for serious drinking—for some.

The bartender greeted Clint like an old friend, magnanimously spreading his arms.

"You're back. Beer?"

"Please."

As the man set the beer down he said, "I wasn't expecting to see you up and around today."

Clint sipped his beer and asked, "Why not?"

"Well, you left with Randy last night, didn't you?"

"Yep."

"Guess you must be one of the few who could ever keep up with her," the bartender said.

Clint decided not to play it coy and said, "Barely."

"I hope she's able to come to work tonight."

"I don't think there'll be a problem with that," Clint said.

"You know," the barman said, "we never properly introduced ourselves. I'm Lee Mosely."

The bartender stuck out his hand and Clint shook it.

"Clint Adams."

"Actually, I know that."

"You do?"

"I asked around."

"Is it generally known that I'm here?"

"Pretty much."

Clint scowled.

"Nobody's gonna bother you here, Mr. Adams," Lee said. "That is, unless some stranger comes ridin' in and finds out you're here."

"Well, I won't be here much longer, anyway."

"Did you find the Reverend?"

"I did."

"Was he who you thought he was?"

"No," Clint lied. It *was* a lie, even though the "Reverend's" identity wasn't assured. Even if he had known for certain that the Reverend Land was J. D. Land, he wouldn't tell anyone. If the man wanted to live a quiet life here as a preacher, who was he to ruin it for him?

So he said, "No, it wasn't him."

"Too bad," Lee said. "Thought maybe you'd found an old friend."

"Not an old friend, but maybe a new one," Clint said. "The Reverend invited me to dinner."

"He does things like that," Lee said. "Invites strangers in town to dinner. He's a real nice fella."

"He seems to be."

"And his wife sure is a good cook."

"You've been out there for dinner?"

"We all have," Lee said. "Coupla times a year they invite the whole town out there and Miriam cooks for them."

"The whole town?"

"Yep."

"That's real generous."

"He's generous with his time," Lee said, "but the town helps out by bringin' the food."

"Sounds fair."

"It is."

"He must be real well liked in this town."

"He sure is," Lee said. "This town wouldn't take too kindly to anybody upsetting him."

Clint wondered if that was just a comment or a warning?

"I'll keep that in mind, Lee."

"And I'll get you another beer on the house," Lee said, taking Clint's empty mug, "seein' as how you're new friends with the Reverend Land."

As the bartender went to get the free beer, Clint wondered why Land hadn't changed his name. If he hadn't kept it, Clint would never have thought twice about leaving Peculiar. If he recognized the name, somebody else might recognize it, too. And it seemed to Clint that J. D. Land used to ride with somebody—a partner. He wondered whatever happened to that man.

"There ya go," Lee said, setting a full, frosty mug down in front of him. "You're makin' new friends all over town, ain't ya? The Reverend. Randy."

"And you," Clint said.

Lee smiled, spread his arms and said, "And me!"

"Why don't you get yourself a drink, Lee," Clint said, "and we'll drink a toast to new friends."

"You got a deal."

ELEVEN

Clint bought himself a new shirt and cleaned his boots for his dinner with the Reverend and his family. He mounted the front porch of the small, wood-frame house and knocked on the door. It was opened by a small boy, maybe seven years of age.

"Who are you?" the boy asked.

"I'm a friend of your daddy's. My name is Clint."

"Pleased to meet you," the boy said, sticking out his little hand. "I'm Joshua, but you can call me Josh."

"Well, hello, Josh," Clint said, shaking the hand. "Is your daddy home?"

"No, sir, but my Mama sure is." The boy turned and ran into the house. "Mama, Mama! A man is here."

As soon as Miriam Land came into view, Clint had no doubt that she knew of her husband's past. It was written on her face as she stared at him, nervously.

"Mr. Adams?"

"That's right. Mrs. Land?"

"Yes. It's . . . nice to meet you."

She was reluctant to invite him into her home. Perhaps she didn't agree with her husband's decision to invite him.

"Uh, I understand from Josh that your husband is not

home yet.'' Clint said. ''I could come back later if you like, when he is?''

''Oh, no, that would be rude of me,'' she said. ''Please, come inside—or have a seat here on the porch and I'll bring you a refreshment.''

''That sounds like a good idea,'' Clint said. There were several wooden chairs on the porch.

''Lemonade?'' she asked. ''I'm afraid I don't have anything stronger.''

''Lemonade would be fine, thank you.''

''I'll be right back.''

Clint sat in one of the chairs to wait. He felt for the woman, who was worried about her husband. The look on her face made him dead sure that he was right, and that the Reverend Land was—or used to be—the gunman J. D. Land.

He heard a sound to his right and saw Josh peering out the open door at him.

''Hello, Josh.''

'Lo.''

''I'm waiting for some lemonade.''

''My Mama makes the best lemonade.''

''Does she? Why don't you ask her to bring you a glass, and you can keep me company.''

The boy's eyes widened and he said, ''Okay!'' and ran back inside, yelling for his mama again.

When Miriam reappeared, she was holding two glasses of lemonade and Josh was right at her side.

''Josh says you invited him to join you?''

''That's right, I did. I thought he and I could talk while you tend to your cooking and we wait for your husband to get home.''

''What do you think of that, Josh?'' his mother asked. ''Would you like to keep Mr. Adams company?''

''You bet,'' the boy said, then added, ''and do I get some lemonade?''

''You certainly do,'' his mother said, and handed him

one of the glasses—the less filled one. The other she gave to Clint.

"Pull up a chair, Josh," Clint said. "Talk to me."

The boy scrambled into a chair enthusiastically, but Clint didn't know if he was enthusiastic to talk or to drink lemonade.

Clint and Josh talked for a half an hour until the Reverend Land appeared, walking up to the house. Clint mostly heard about school and the boy's friends. He was convinced that Josh would talk his ear off, given half a chance.

"Well," Land said, good naturedly, "looks like you two are getting along."

"We're havin' lemonade, Papa."

"And it looks good, too," Land said. "Why don't I go inside and say hello to your mother and then I'll come out and have some with you?"

"Okay!"

"We'll wait here," Clint said. "Josh was telling me about his friend, Chuckie."

"Chuckie," Land repeated, then went inside, shaking his head.

"What does your pa have against Chuckie?" Clint asked Josh.

"Chuckie and his ma and pa don't come to church," Josh said.

"I see."

"That don't matter to me, 'cause Chuckie's still my friend," the boy said, "but it matters to Pa."

"Well," Clint said, "I think it matters to your pa because that's his job, Josh."

"I guess. At least he doesn't tell me *not* to play with Chuckie."

"Sounds like your pa wants to let you make up your own mind about your friends."

Josh thought that over and then said, "Yeah, I guess you're right."

At that moment the Reverend Land came out carrying a glass of lemonade.

"Josh, why don't you go inside and help your ma set the table, and I'll talk to Mr. Adams for a little while."

"All right, Pa." The boy got down from the chair.

"It was nice talking to you, Josh."

"Nice talking to you, too, sir."

As Land took the chair his son had vacated, Clint said, "That's a bright, well-mannered boy, Reverend."

"Thank you," Land said. "That's due mostly to his ma."

"I'm sure you've had something to do with it."

"Maybe."

They sat and drank lemonade in silence for a while and then—as if the question had been trying to burst out of him—John David Land said, "You do know who I am, don't you?"

Clint thought about lying, but decided against it.

"I suspected who you were," he said, "yes."

"Who are you going to tell?"

"No one."

"Why not?"

"Because the man you were is far behind you," Clint said. "If I wanted to tell anyone anything it would be about the man you are now."

"That's very decent of you."

"Answer me one thing, though."

"What's that?"

"Why didn't you change your name?"

"Because God called me under my own name," Land said. "I couldn't change it after that."

"I see," Clint said. "And your wife? Does she know everything?"

"Of course," Land said. "I couldn't very well expect

her to marry me without knowing the truth, could I?"

"Of course not."

"She knows about my past and loves me anyway," Land said, "as does God."

"I thought God loves everybody."

Land looked at Clint for a long moment before answering.

"You're not a church-going man, are you, Mr. Adams?"

"No."

"Do you believe in the existence of God."

"Let's put it this way," Clint said. "After everything I've seen, if there is a God, he's got a hell of a lot of explaining to do."

"To you?"

"To everyone."

"God doesn't owe any of us an explanation," Land said. "It's we who owe him an explanation for our actions, and we owe him our gratitude—"

"Sorry, Reverend," Clint said, cutting the man off, "but you're barking up the wrong tree. I don't begrudge you your beliefs, but don't expect me to be grateful to God for the things he has visited on me—if he exists."

"Perhaps while you're here I can convince you—"

"Reverend," Clint said, "I try to make it a policy never to discuss religion." The other policy he lived by was never to pay for a woman, but he didn't mention that.

"You blame God because you've had to live by your gun?"

"I thought I came here for supper," Clint said, "not a sermon."

"My husband is big on sermons, Mr. Adams," Miriam Land said from the door. "You're finding out what everyone in town already knows."

''I'm sure he is, Mrs. Land,'' Clint said. ''It's just that . . . well, I'm not.''

''Well then,'' she said, ''perhaps you gentlemen would like to come inside and have some supper?''

''We'd love to, Miriam,'' Land said.

TWELVE

As promised, Miriam Land was a wonderful cook. She roasted beef to perfection, garnished it with vegetables and prepared a pecan pie for dessert. In addition, her coffee was good and strong, the way Clint liked it.

"Keeps me awake at night when I have a sermon to write," Land said, later, on the porch again.

After Josh helped his mama clear the table, it was time for him to say goodnight to his pa and Clint.

"Will you be here tomorrow, Clint?" he asked.

"I'm afraid not, Josh," Clint said. "I really have to get going. But it was a real pleasure to meet you."

"It was a pleasure to meet you, too."

Clint put his hand out for the boy to shake, but Josh surprised him by giving him a big hug.

"Bye," the boy said, and ran inside.

"You're a hit with my son," Land said.

"It's nice to be a hit with somebody," Clint said.

"You're a hit with God," Land said. "Everybody is."

"Not everybody, Reverend."

"But you see—"

"I appreciate the supper and the hospitality, Reverend,'' Clint said, cutting him off, ''but I really don't want to get into this kind of discussion.''

''Very well,'' Land said. ''You're a guest in my house, so I will respect your wishes.''

''I would like to know one thing, though.''

''And what's that?''

''Why a preacher?'' Clint asked. ''Out of all the things you could have been, or could have done—''

''You speak as if I had a choice,'' Land said.

''Didn't you?''

''No, not at all.''

''But why not?''

''Because, as I told you before, I was called to this,'' Land said. ''When the Lord calls you, you answer.''

''Guess I've never gotten that call,'' Clint said. ''I just thought maybe you decided to do something totally the opposite of what you had been doing.''

''That ends up being the case, although it wasn't my intent.''

''Didn't you have a partner riding with you?'' Clint asked. ''I seem to remember somebody—''

''Arnold Pace,'' Land said.

''That's right! Now I remember. Arnie Pace. He went on to make a name for himself.''

''As a criminal,'' Land said, ''and a killer.''

''And a fast gun.''

''Poor Arnie,'' the Reverend said.

''Why poor?''

''He always wondered who was faster, him or me.''

''It was never put to the test?''

''No.''

''Why not?''

''I wasn't interested in finding out.''

''What if he came around now?'' Clint asked. ''What if he rode into this town and heard about a preacher named Land? What then?''

"I would have to face him without the benefit of a gun."

"Where is your gun, Reverend?" Clint asked. "Or should I say, where is J. D. Land's gun?"

"I . . . got rid of it," Land said. "It's gone. My only weapon now is the bible."

"And are you as lethal with it as you were with your gun?" Clint asked.

"Well, judging by my inability to sway you," Land said, looking amused, "I'm afraid not."

Their conversation was interrupted when Miriam Land came out to join them.

"Is Josh asleep?" Land asked.

"Yes. Mr. Adams?"

"Yes, Ma'am?"

"May I ask you a question?"

"Of course."

"I don't know what you and my husband have talked about, but you are aware of who he is, are you not?"

Clint looked at Land for a moment and then said, "Yes, Ma'am, I am."

"May I ask what you intend to do with that information?"

"Well, Mrs. Land, I don't intend to do anything with it," he said. "Tomorrow I intend to ride out of Peculiar and forget that it, and you, ever existed—although your pecan pie will be a little hard to forget."

She put her hand on her husband's arm and squeezed. "We're very happy here."

"I can see that, Ma'am," Clint said, "and I would never do anything to jeopardize that. Please believe me."

"I do believe you, Mr. Adams," she said. "And I thank you."

THIRTEEN

After Miriam turned in for the night—kissing her husband lightly on the lips and Clint on the cheek—Clint and Land talked a while longer on the porch. The Reverend no longer tried to convert Clint, but asked questions about what was going on in the world.

"We're very isolated here," he explained. "We don't have a newspaper yet, and we don't get a lot of strangers riding through."

"That doesn't sound like a bad thing," Clint said. "In fact, it sounds like a good place to settle down, especially if you don't want anyone to find you."

"Would you like to do that, Clint?"

"Settle here?"

"Settle anywhere."

"I've tried it," Clint said. "It doesn't work for me, Reverend."

"Please," Land said, "call me John."

"I tried once or twice, John, to leave it behind, but it always manages to find me again, so I've accepted my fate."

"To meet it at the end of a gun?"

"Perhaps," Clint said. "After all, I don't know too many men who lived by their gun who didn't die by it."

"And you accept that as your end?"

"My probable end, yes."

Land studied Clint for a few moments, and then said, "I sense that you're at peace with that."

"I am."

"How odd. I wonder if I could have ever accepted that if I hadn't turned to God," the Reverend said.

"Lucky for you," Clint said, "you'll never have to know."

Before leaving, Clint had one last question for the Reverend John David Land.

"What would it take for you to pick up a gun again, John?"

Land thought the question over for a few moments, and then said, "A miracle, Clint."

Clint rode away from the house feeling uneasy, because, after all, weren't miracles the business the Reverend Land was in?

FOURTEEN

One month later . . .

The Reverend John David Land was no more. The man who stood before the burned out house, cold on the outside while burning on the inside, was once again J. D. Land.

Next to him stood Andy Worth, who had recognized Land the moment he'd ridden into town ten years ago, and kept the secret all these years.

"John David—"

"Don't call me that anymore."

Worth hesitated, then said, "J. D., you haven't picked up a gun in ten years. What makes you think you can just take up where you left off?"

"I don't have a choice, Andy."

"Sure you do," he said. "Would Miriam have wanted the rest of your life to be consumed by vengeance?"

Land turned his cold eyes on Andy Worth, who shivered.

"It won't take me the rest of my life to find them."

"Why not?"

"Because I know who they are."

"How could you know that?"

"Because two descriptions mentioned one man who had a v-shaped scar on his left cheek."

"And?"

"Arnie Pace has that scar."

"Did he have it ten years ago?" Worth asked. "I mean, how can you know if he has—"

"I gave him that scar ten years ago."

That quieted the sheriff, and he simply watched as J. D. Land circled the house, studying the burned-out husk and the ground, as if they would tell him something.

"What about tracking?" Worth asked. "You ain't tracked so much as a deer since you came here."

"That's something else you don't forget."

Although Worth knew who Land was—or had been—it was odd to see the Reverend wearing a gun, and wearing it as if he knew how to use it.

Land finished walking around what was left of the house and came to a stop in front of Worth.

"The tracks lead north," he said. "That's where I'm headed."

"I guess all I have to say is good luck."

Land studied Worth for a few moments.

"How long have you known?"

"I've always known."

"And you kept quiet all these years?"

"Yes."

"Why?"

"Because you deserved a chance to start over," Worth said, "and you were doing good things for this town. Then, when you married Miriam, the transformation was complete."

"And now," Land said, "I've transformed back."

"John—J. D.," Worth said. "Let me come with you."

"No," Land said, "this is for me to do."

"Do you think that Pace knew that this was your home, your family?" the lawman asked.

"Oh, he knew," Land said. "Arnie Pace never does anything without a good reason."

"So you're going to track him, and three or four other men, and then face them alone?"

"Yes."

"Do you want to die?"

Land looked his friend in the eye and said, "Yes . . . but not until they do."

Land mounted the big Morgan horse he'd bought for stamina and rode away, without so much as a wave or a look back. Worth thought about following him, but he was the sheriff of Peculiar, and he did not have a deputy. He could not just up and leave, especially when Land didn't want him along. So he stood there until his friend was out of sight and then mounted his own horse and rode back to town.

FIFTEEN

Clint was in St. Louis when the telegram reached him. It was from Rick Hartman in Denver, and it informed him that a lawman named Andy Worth, from a town called Peculiar, in Missouri, was looking for him. Clint, in turn, tried to send a telegram to Andy Worth in Peculiar, but the town did not have its own telegraph key. He asked the operator in the St. Louis office for the name of the closest town to Peculiar that *did* have a key, and then sent the telegram there.

His reply came several hours later, delivered to his hotel. He sat on the bed in his room and read it.

LAND FAMILY KILLED. REVERED IS J. D. AGAIN. NEEDS HELP. HEADING NORTH, HUNTING ARNIE PACE.

SHERIFF ANDY WORTH

Clint couldn't believe it. Not only Miriam, but the boy, too? That bright, respectful, lively boy? Who would do such a thing? Well, the answer to that was in the telegram, wasn't it? Somehow, Land's old partner Arnie Pace had found him, and instead of taking his revenge on him, took it on his family. That was the miracle John David Land had been talking about, the one that would make him pick up a gun again, that would turn him into J. D. Land again.

How do you feel about your God now, J. D.? Clint wondered.

According to the telegram from Andy Worth, J. D. Land would be riding north. If he didn't cross the Mississippi at some point he would eventually come to St. Louis. But Clint couldn't count on that, so he saddled Duke, said goodbye to his friends in St. Louis, and started south, hoping to run into the reborn gunman.

How much would ten years without holding a gun erode his own skills, he wondered? What made Land think he could just pick it up again. Then again, if his family was dead, he probably *wasn't* thinking clearly. He was being driven now by a higher power than the God who had called him. Vengeance had called him, and now *it* was his god, demanding obedience, and respect, and loyalty. It had a hunger and was demanding to be fed, and when J. D. Land found Arnie Pace and his men, it would be—but what price would Land pay?

He liked the Reverend John David Land and his family, even after spending only one evening with them. He felt an ache in his heart when he thought of that little boy, so what must Land himself be feeling?

What, indeed.

"What makes you think he's gonna follow us?" Paxton Lewis asked Arnie Pace while the rest of the men looked on.

"Oh, he'll follow," Pace said.

"How's he gonna know it was you?" Pax asked. "Or us."

"This," Pace said, touching the V-shaped scar on his cheek, "this will tell him it's me."

"I don't know, Arnie," Pax said. "I remember the

stories about J. D. Land. Why would you want to wake him up again?''

''First of all,'' Pace said, glaring across the campfire at his partner, ''I was always faster than Land with a gun. Don't forget that.''

''Sure, Arnie,'' Pax said, ''I won't forget.''

''And he's been away from his gun a long time,'' Pace said. ''It ain't gonna come back to him that easy.''

''I'll never understand how you could have waited this long,'' Pax said. ''Hell, you knew he was there three, four years ago.''

''Longer,'' Pace said, ''a lot longer.''

''So how come you didn't go there before this?''

''Because,'' Arnie Pace said, ''I wanted him comfortable and happy before I took everything away from him. I wanted to be sure that he'd come lookin' for me after I was done.''

''And you're sure he is?''

''Dead sure.''

''How can you be so sure?''

''There are things inside a man that don't change,'' Pace said. ''This will be the only solution for him, to pick up his gun and come and get me.''

''And then what?''

''And then,'' Arnie Pace said, ''I'll kill him and finish the job.''

J. D. Land felt odd sitting in the saddle again, riding alone. He hadn't been alone for ten years, and now that he was again, it felt much worse than he remembered. Of course, he realized that it wasn't just being alone that felt bad, it was being without Miriam and the boy.

He tried to work up his anger again at their slaughter, but at that moment could not. He knew, though, that the anger had only abated. It would not go away until he had expiated it by the act of vengeance. That would take care of Arnie Pace and his men.

And then he would plot his vengeance against God.

SIXTEEN

As Clint rode north he realized that this plan was hit or miss. Either he'd run into Land along the way, or they would totally miss each other. There had to be a way to take out some insurance. He decided to stop at the next town or city with a telegraph and send a wire to Rick Hartman. The town turned out to be Hermann.

REQUESTING INFORMATION ON WHEREABOUTS OF ARNIE PACE.

CLINT

He remained in Hermann the rest of the day, hoping that an answer would come in. He knew if he left Hermann without the answer, Rick wouldn't be able to track him down.

Luckily, while Clint was in a café eating German food—Hermann had been settled by Germans—the telegraph operator brought him his answer.

ARNIE PACE SPOTTED IN ILLINOIS. HEADING NORTH. MY INFORMATION SAYS HE'S HEADING FOR MINNESOTA.

RICK H.

Clint shook his head. He didn't know how Rick got his information, but it was usually pretty good. Now he had a choice. Keep moving north through Illinois toward Minnesota, or stay in Missouri until he reached Iowa. Land had the advantage of tracking the killers. Clint was going to have to make up his mind one way or the other which way to go.

In the end he decided to head through Illinois, aiming for Minnesota. If Land was any good, he'd reach there as well. And maybe Clint could find Pace first, because he knew if Land did, there wouldn't be any way for the man to go back to God when he was done.

Arnie Pace and his right arm, Paxton Lewis, usually sat away from the other three men.

"I don't know about Minnesota," Pax said. "Why are we heading there?"

"Why not?"

"It's cold."

"Good," Pace said. "I want J. D. to be cold. He always hated the cold more than anything."

"You know him pretty well, huh?" Pax asked.

"Better than he knows himself."

Pax didn't understand that. He didn't know anyone that well.

"So when we meet up with him he's gonna be cold *and* mad," Pax said. "Don't sound like a good combination, Arnie."

"It will be," Pace said. "I've seen J. D. in action, Pax. He has to be cold and unemotional to be effective. Do you think he'll be unemotional when he sees me?"

"Not a chance."

"Exactly," Pace said. "I've taken that away from him. Little by little, I'll take everything he has . . . and then I'll take his life. Or maybe it will be even crueler to leave him alive."

He'd make his final decision when the time came.

Clint had been in Minnesota with the James Boys some years ago and had not been back since. Even as he crossed the border it seemed to get colder. He pulled out a fur-lined jacket he'd bought for the trip and slipped it on. It wasn't something he often wore in the Southwest, where he seemed to spend most of his time, and he found it somewhat confining. If he needed to get at his gun he would have to open it again.

But he doubted he'd be needing his gun anytime soon, especially not while he was alone in the Minnesota woods.

He camped soon after he crossed into Minnesota, building himself a large enough fire to both cook on and to generate heat from. Over coffee and beans he wondered why Arnie Pace would head for Minnesota. Did he come from there? Was he trying to lure J. D. Land onto his home turf?

After he ate he wrapped himself in his blanket and tried to get some sleep. The ground was hard and unyielding, and it was not yet winter. He didn't fancy ever seeing how cold it got here in the dead of winter. This was cold enough for him. Idly he wondered how J. D. Land felt about the cold.

J. D. Land pulled a second blanket around him and moved closer to the fire, but it seemed to do little against the bone-chilling cold. Arnie Pace knew he hated the cold, that was why he was leading him up here. But Pace was forgetting that Land knew him at least as well as he knew Land. He knew Arnie's plan. He figured it out during the long hours in the saddle since he'd left Peculiar. Arnie was trying to demoralize him, taking his family, leading him to Minnesota where it was cold. Arnie was doing everything he could to see that he had an edge when they met.

This was why Land was not in a hurry, was not pushing his horse beyond its endurance, was not traveling at night. Arnie Pace *wanted* to be found, and that was all right with Land. All he had to do when they met was control his temper. It was all right to feel the hate, but he couldn't let it get in the way of his vengeance. The vengeance came first, and then—over the dead body of his ex-partner—he could allow the hate to come out.

But he had no idea what he would do after that. He couldn't go back to Peculiar. That just wasn't a place he could be anymore. Neither would he be able to go back to the church—not after what he was going to do. And anyway, he wouldn't *want* to go back, not after God allowed his family to die.

He remembered what Clint Adams had told him when asked if he believed in God. He'd said something about "having a lot to explain" if he exists.

John David Land did not agree with that at the time.

But J. D. Land now did.

Clint thought he smelled another campfire. How much of a coincidence would it be if that fire belonged to J. D. Land? He hated to think of coincidences, so he decided to consider it as a possibly fortuitous occurrence. After all, they had both headed for Minnesota from Missouri, right?

The smell came from downwind, which meant that the smell of Clint's fire would not be noticed. He decided that in the morning, when the sun came out and it was not so cold, he would check it out.

It was just too damned cold to do anything now.

SEVENTEEN

The next morning Clint rolled out of his blanket and stoked his fire. He wasn't going anywhere until he had coffee. He walked away from his fire and sniffed the air. Satisfied that he could still smell the other campfire, he put a pot of coffee over the flame and waited.

J. D. Land prepared his coffee, then decided to cook some of the bacon he had brought with him. It wasn't because he was hungry, or because he liked bacon, but because he wanted to keep his strength up. When he caught up to Arnie he was going to have to be at his best, because Arnie would be at his—and Arnie would have at least three or four other men with him. Facing five men didn't bother Land. As long as he killed Arnie, he'd be happy, even if he ended up dead himself.

As long as Arnie died first, so he could see it.

Sam Perry started a pot of coffee and then woke the others, since he'd had the last watch.

"Where's the coffee?" Arnie Pace asked.

"It's almost ready, Arnie."

Arnie Pace brought his fist down onto Perry's boot toe. The man howled and hopped around.

"How many times I got to tell you not to wake me until the coffee's ready?" Pace demanded.

"Ow, ow, ow, I'm sorry, Arnie, ow . . ."

"Get me a goddamned cup!"

"Ow . . . comin' up . . . ow . . ."

Pax came up next to Arnie and sniffed the air.

"You smell that?"

"What? The coffee?" Pace asked.

"No," Pax said, "someone else's."

Pace sniffed the air, then walked away from the campfire and sniffed at the air again.

"Somebody has a camp near here," he said.

"That's what I think."

Pace turned back to Pax.

"Send Jimmy Boy out there to see what's going on."

"Right."

Pax went to tell Jimmy Smith—who Pace always called "Jimmy Boy" because of his youth—to mount up and ride out.

"There's somebody out there with a camp going," he said. "Find out who."

"I ain't had my breakfast, yet," Jimmy whined.

"You can have it when you come back."

"It'll probably be all gone by then, the way you guys eat."

"I tell you what," Pax said, "when you find whoever it is, kill them and eat their breakfast."

"All right!" Jimmy Boy said, and went to saddle his horse.

"Have you ever seen such a bloodthirsty youngster before?" Pax asked Arnie Pace.

Pace thought back to the days he rode with the young J. D. Land and said, "Yeah, I have."

EIGHTEEN

After breakfast, Clint saddled Duke, collected his belongings and stomped out the fire. Then he mounted up and went looking for the source of that other campfire.

He traveled slowly, making a minimum of noise himself while stopping every so often to listen. Finally, he heard someone moving through the woods, coming toward him. He dismounted and walked Duke into cover and waited there. Soon, a rider came into view . . .

When Jimmy Boy rode back to camp he said, "I couldn't find nothin'."

Arnie Pace and Paxton exchanged glances that said the kid was lying, that he had rushed back to make sure he got some breakfast.

"How hard did you try?" Pace asked.

"I tried hard, Arnie," Jimmy said, dismounting. "Any breakfast left?"

"Not for you, there ain't," Pace said.

"What?" The younger man looked distraught.

"You go back out there and don't come back until you've found someone," Pace ordered.

"But Arnie—"

"Do like you're told, Jimmy," Pax said. "You can eat later."

Perry looked at the other men, who were sitting there enjoying their breakfasts and the fact that they weren't being yelled at.

"Well?" Pace asked. "Are you part of this gang or not?"

"Sure I am!" Jimmy Boy said.

"Then get out there and do your part, Jimmy Boy."

The young man kicked at the ground and then said, "Yes, sir." He mounted up and rode back out again.

"He'll learn," Paxton told Pace.

"Maybe," Arnie Pace said, "he'll learn the hard way."

Miranda Holt was lost. She didn't know what direction to go in to reach the nearest town, and her horse—which she had bought in Wisconsin—was no help at all.

She was cold and hungry. All she'd been able to prepare at her campfire the night before was coffee. She'd had one piece of beef jerky left and had eaten it that morning for breakfast. Now all she could think about was a thick steak, and it was driving her crazy.

When she saw the man riding up to her she didn't know what to think. She panicked and pulled her rifle from its scabbard. Not very good with a gun, she got her finger stuck in the trigger guard and accidentally fired it.

Clint heard the shot and decided not to wait. He mounted Duke and rode in the direction of the shot. When he reached the source he saw a man and a woman struggling on horseback, over a rifle. He had no choice but to deal himself in.

When Jimmy Boy saw the woman he realized she was going for her gun. He rode up to her quickly as the rifle went off, firing into the ground. By this time he reached her and grabbed hold of the gun.

"Let go!" she shouted.

"You let go!"

"I won't!"

And they struggled for it. Finally, Jimmy Boy pushed her from the saddle. She fell to the ground with a loud thud and cried out as her butt hit the hard-packed earth.

Jimmy Boy, seeing his chance, reversed her rifle and aimed it at her. He enjoyed killing even more than he enjoyed women.

"Hold it!" Clint yelled.

Jimmy Boy froze just for an instant, then turned with the rifle. Clint had no choice but to draw a fire, which he did. Jimmy Boy Smith went flying from his saddle and was dead when he hit the ground.

"Jesus!" Miranda said.

Clint dismounted and walked over to her.

"Are you all right?"

"I think so," she said. "I think my butt might be broke."

"Just stay there a minute," he said, and went to check the man he'd shot.

"Is he dead?"

"He's dead, all right."

He came back to her, reached out a hand and helped her up.

"How did you do that?" she asked.

"Do what?"

"He had you," she said. "He turned with his rifle and he had you, but you still drew and shot him."

"He hesitated a half a second."

"Maybe, but is half a second enough time to kill a man?"

"Apparently," he said. He dropped the spent shell from the cylinder, inserted a live one and holstered the gun.

"How's your butt?" he asked.

She turned and showed him an extremely shapely butt, clad in jeans. She rubbed it with both hands.

"Feels sore," she said, "but I think I'll live. Who was that man?"

"I don't know," he said. "I thought you knew him."

"No," she said, "I just sort of rode up on him, and I guess I panicked. I grabbed for my rifle and it went off into the ground."

"Well, it's a good thing it did," he said, "otherwise I might not have found you in time."

Her eyes got wide—big, pretty brown eyes—and she said, "He was gonna shoot me in cold blood!" Her face was pretty, too, but it was difficult to see how she was built because of her jacket.

"That's how it looked."

"Jesus, Mister," she said, "you saved my life."

"Glad I could help. Let's see if we can find out who he is. You go through his saddlebags, and I'll go through his pockets."

"Okay."

"Wait," he said, "First, what's your name?"

She hesitated a moment, then said, "Miranda." It sounded as if she was going to add a last name, but decided against it.

"Pleased to meet you, Miranda. I'm Clint."

They each went about their respective tasks. Clint found a letter in the dead man's shirt pocket addressed to Jimmy Smith. Miranda found another one in his saddlebag, also addressed to Jimmy Smith.

"Well," Clint said, after they had compared notes, "meet Mister Jimmy Smith."

"Any idea *who* he was?" she asked.

"None."

"Me neither."

"Where were you headed?" Clint asked.

"Actually, I was lost—or am lost. I was just trying

to get to the nearest town. I'm out of supplies."

"Well, the closest town is Deerfield," Clint said. "I was headed there myself. If we go together, maybe we'll find out something about this fella."

"That sounds fine to me," Miranda said, "but what do we do with him? His body, I mean?"

"We take him with us," Clint said. "We don't want any misunderstandings with the law."

"I guess not."

"I'll tie him to his horse, and we can be on our way."

"All right."

She watched while Clint tied the body onto his horse, then they both mounted up. Clint decided he would lead the horse and gave Miranda directions on how to get to Deerfield.

"You've been up this way before," she said.

"Once or twice."

"Doubly lucky for me, then, that you came along."

"And pretty unlucky for this fella," Clint said.

"Well," Miranda replied, "all I can say is, better him than me."

NINETEEN

When Arnie Pace, Paxton and the others reached the spot where Jimmy Boy had been shot, they dismounted.

"Blood on the ground," Paxton said.

"Have a look around," Pace told the other two men. "See what you can find."

"Right, Arnie," Bruce Roberts said. He looked at Ted Lowell and said, "Come on."

They had heard the shot while breaking camp and went in search of the source.

While Lowell and Roberts looked around in the woods, Pace and Paxton examined the hard ground.

"Look here," Pax said, crouching down and pointing.

"Is that a hoofprint?"

"Just enough of one to know that it was made by Jimmy's horse."

"Then what happened to him?" Pace asked.

"That must be his blood," Pax said. "Maybe he's hurt."

"Or dead."

Pax stood up and looked around some more.

"Arnie?

"Yeah?"

"Take a look."

Pace joined his partner and looked down at the ground. There were drops in the dirt.

"Whoever was bleeding still is," Pax said. "We can follow this trail, but . . ."

"But what?"

"Well . . . what if it's Land?"

"Can't be," Pace said.

"Why not?"

"He would have to have been ahead of us, and that just can't be."

"But maybe—"

"It wasn't Land, believe me. He wouldn't waste his time with Jimmy Boy. He's comin' after me."

"Well, somethin' happened here."

"And we'll follow this trail of blood and see where it leads us."

"What if it's not Jimmy's blood?" Pax asked. "What if it's somebody else's?"

"Well, I guess we'll find that out when we get where we're goin'," Pace said. "Get the other two, Pax. I want to get started."

"Right."

Arnie Pace stood looking at the blood on the ground. Jimmy Boy was no big loss, but he *was* part of the Pace gang, and they couldn't afford to have people thinking they could just shoot members of the gang and get away with it.

As for Pax's question about J. D. Land, he still felt there was no way in hell that J. D. could have gotten ahead of them. And even if he had, he wouldn't have known that Jimmy was part of the gang. Probably the best explanation of what had happened was that Jimmy Boy ran into something that panicked him, and it got him killed.

It was a lucky thing that there was no paper out on Jimmy, and nothing to tie him to Arnie Pace and his gang. Still, this had to be looked into, like it or not. Jimmy was, after all, one of them.

TWENTY

When Clint and Miranda rode into Deerfield with the dead body slung over the saddle, they attracted a lot of attention. Miranda began to fidget.

"What's wrong?" Clint asked.

"Nothing," she said. "I just don't like having people stare at me."

"Why don't you go to the livery and put up your horse, and then get a hotel room?" he suggested.

"And what are you gonna do?"

"I'll stop at the sheriff's office and try to get rid of this body."

"All right," she agreed, readily. "I'll see you at the hotel later, then."

"Fine."

She started away, then turned back.

"I just have to say thanks one more time, Clint," she said. "You kept me alive, and kept me from wandering aimlessly in the woods for days. I really do appreciate it."

"I'll tell you what. When I'm finished with the sheriff, you can show me how much you appreciate it."

"What?" She eyed him suspiciously.

"No, no," he said, putting her fears aside, "I meant

you could buy me a drink, or some lunch.''

''Lunch sounds good,'' she said. ''I'll see you at, uh, that hotel over there. The Deerfield House.''

''The Deerfield House it is,'' he agreed, and they separated.

As Clint approached the sheriff's office, a man wearing a badge came out and stood there, waiting for him. The sheriff's thumbs were hooked into his gunbelt, and the position thrust his pot belly forward. As Clint came closer, the man appeared to be in his fifties.

''You look like you're waiting for me, Sheriff,'' Clint said, dismounting.

''You get so you can feel when the town is agitated,'' the man said. He walked to the body and examined it, satisfying himself that the man was dead, then looked up at Clint. ''Also helps to have a deputy who saw you ride in and came running to tell me about it''

Clint instantly liked the man.

''Who is this fella?'' the lawman asked.

''I was hoping you'd tell me that.''

''You kill him?''

''Yes.''

''Why?''

''He aimed a rifle at me,'' Clint said. ''He was about to kill a woman with it. I stopped him.''

''Lucky for her,'' the sheriff said, as a deputy came out of the office. ''That the dead man's horse?''

''Yes.''

He turned to the deputy and said, ''Hiram, take the body over to the undertaker's and the horse to the livery.''

''Right Sheriff.''

''This is all we got off him,'' Clint said, handing the sheriff the letters they had each found.

The sheriff studied them and then stuffed them in his shirt pocket.

"Well, at least we've got a name. I'll check and see if there's any paper on him."

"I don't want any reward if there is. I'm not a bounty hunter."

"By the way," the sheriff said, "who are you?"

"My name's Clint Adams."

Clint went to the hotel to check in and then find Miranda.

"The lady who checked in before me," he said to the clerk. "Is she in her room?"

"Lady?"

"Yes," Clint said, "a young lady—wait."

He looked at the register again and saw that his was the first signature in it in three days.

"That's strange."

"Sir?"

"No woman checked in just before me?"

"No, sir."

"Is there another hotel in town?"

"No, sir," the clerk said, "but there's a rooming house."

Clint doubted that Miranda would have preferred a rooming house, but he got directions from the man and went to check.

After he'd introduced himself to the sheriff, the man had tried not to look impressed. He told Clint to get himself settled and they'd talk later. He also said he wanted to talk to the woman Clint had saved from being killed. Clint had told him that would not be a problem.

Now he wasn't so sure.

Miranda had not gone to the rooming house, so Clint's next stop was the livery. When he'd left Duke off there he hadn't bothered to ask about a woman. When he did ask, and described her to the liveryman, the liveryman shook his head.

"There weren't no woman here," the man said.

"There had to be," Clint said. "I rode in with her. We split up and she rode over here."

"Mister," the older man said, "I think your misses rode right on out of town."

"She's not my wife."

"Girlfriend, then. That happens, sometimes, you know? Ya can't keep a woman happy for long. It just ain't natural."

"Thanks," Clint said, and left.

He walked around town and an hour later still could not find Miranda anywhere. If she had left town, why would she do it? What was she afraid of? And now that she was gone, the sheriff only had his word that he killed Jim Smith in self-defense. Miranda was going to back up his story.

Clint decided to take the bull by the horns and walked over to the sheriff's office.

"Gone?" the lawman asked. "What do you mean, gone?"

"Apparently, she left town."

"You just got to town."

"I know that."

"Why would she do that?"

"That I don't know."

The sheriff's name was Townsend, Charles Townsend. The deputy called him Charlie.

"I've got a dead man at the undertaker's, Adams, and only your word you killed him in self-defense—and in defense of a woman who isn't even here now."

"I realize that, Sheriff," Clint said, "but why would I ride into town and make up a story like that? And if I killed him for some other reason, why would I bring him into town?"

"All of that's valid," the sheriff said, "but this

woman has disappeared—if she ever existed. What was her name?''

''Miranda.''

''Miranda what?''

''I never got a last name.''

''And you only just met her?''

''Actually,'' Clint said, ''we introduced ourselves after the man was dead.''

''Did you tell her your full name?''

Clint frowned, then said, ''I don't think so. No. Why?''

''Well, you have a reputation,'' Sheriff Townsend said. ''I thought maybe that might have frightened her away.''

''That's possible, I guess,'' Clint said, ''but to the best of my recollection, we only exchanged first names.''

''Well, I still haven't found out anything about the dead man. If I do, I'll send Chad here to your hotel for you''

Chad was the young deputy, and at the sound of his name he stood up.

''Sit down, Chad.''

The deputy sat.

''I'll go back to my hotel, then,'' Clint said.

''One thing before you go,'' Townsend said.

''What's that?''

The sheriff put out his hand and said, ''I'll need your gun.''

Clint faced the sheriff squarely and said, ''We have a problem then.''

TWENTY-ONE

"What do you mean?" the sheriff asked.

"I can't give you my gun, Sheriff," Clint said. "That would make me a target. I can't go around unarmed, especially since we don't know who this man was. He might have friends in town."

"He doesn't have any friends in town," Sheriff Townsend said, "because he's not from here."

"That may be so, but I still can't go around unarmed."

"Nobody knows who you are."

"You do," Clint said and then jerked his thumb at Chad and said, "your deputy does. And so does the clerk in the hotel. Believe me, word will get around. It always does."

"I need your gun, Adams, to make sure everyone in my town is safe," Townsend said.

"You have my word, Sheriff, that I'm not looking to shoot anyone in your town," Clint replied. "I simply can't give you my gun."

"And what if I try to take it?"

"All I have to say to that is, please don't."

Townsend matched stares with Clint and, then said to the deputy, "Chad, get out."

"And do what?" the young man asked, getting to his feet.

"Don't you have rounds to do?"

"Well, yeah, later, but—"

"Go do them now."

"Yes, sir."

Chad collected his hat and went out the door, but not before taking a curious glance back. He wondered what he was going to miss.

"I wanted him out of here so he didn't hear this," Townsend said. "It might give him the wrong idea."

"What might?"

"The fact that I'm going to let you keep your gun," Townsend said. "See, I don't think I can take it from you—not with you being who you are and all. I didn't want the boy to see me back down."

"Sheriff," Clint said, "my aim is not to back you down, it's to stay alive. I've been keeping myself alive for a long time now, and believe me, not being in public without my gun is one way I do it."

"I can appreciate that," the lawman said. "Are you at the Deerfield House?"

"Yes."

"Where were you on your way to when all of this happened?"

"I'm trying to find somebody who is supposed to be in Minnesota."

"Who?"

"Arnie Pace."

"I know the name," Townsend said. "Do you think the man you killed was one of Pace's gang?"

"I have no way of knowing that," Clint said, "but if he is, then I was a lot closer than I thought."

"And if they're that close, they might be coming here," Townsend said. "That would be a good reason for you to leave town."

"Before you find out who the dead man really is? Without locating my witness, the gi—"

"None if that is as important as getting you out of town before Pace and his men get here."

"And if they do come here, you'll face them?"

"That's my job."

"Alone?"

"I've got a deputy."

"So just you and Chad, huh?"

"If we have to."

"I could stick around and help," Clint said. "I've never seen Pace, and he's never seen me."

"You don't want to help me," Townsend said. "You just want to wait for Pace so you don't have to chase him. What's he done to you anyway?"

"He killed the family of a friend of mine," Clint said. "A wife and a seven-year-old boy."

"Jesus," the lawman said, shaking his head, "no wonder you want him, but I still can't let my town become a shooting zone. I'll give you today to get rested, but tomorrow morning I'd like you to leave town."

"Well, Sheriff," Clint said, "luckily, we don't have a problem then. I'll be out shortly after first light."

"And I'll hold you to your word not to shoot anyone tonight."

Sheriff, I promise you," Clint said, "that I won't shoot anybody who doesn't try to shoot me first."

As Clint Adams left his office, Sheriff Charlie Townsend figured that was the best he was going to get him the Gunsmith.

Instead of going back to the hotel, Clint decided to stop in the saloon and have a beer. As soon as he walked in, though, he became aware that people were staring at him. Apparently, word had gotten out even quicker than he'd thought, and everyone knew who he was. One beer, he told himself, and out.

Of course, there's always someone who has other plans.

The news had quickly gotten around town of the Gunsmith's presence, due mainly to the big mouth of Deputy Chad Wright. After leaving the sheriff's office he ran around like the town crier, telling anybody who'd listen that the Gunsmith was in town.

Bodie Jessup had found that information very interesting. At thirty years old, Bodie was feeling his oats. He was a big man, in the pink of health, powerfully built and convinced that there wasn't a man alive who could take him in a fair fight.

He was also convinced that his prowess with a gun would soon make him famous. He was quick to get his gun out of his holster, and accurate with it once he did. He had everything it took to become the greatest shootist of all time.

In his own opinion, of course.

Bodie was sitting at a table with his two friends, Tim Shockley—whom he called "Shock"—and Abner Clay, when Clint Adams came walking in.

"There he is," Bodie said, "the big, bad Gunsmith."

"He don't look so bad, Bodie," Clay said.

"You can take him easy," Shock said.

"He's kinda old, too," Clay said. "It don't look like you're gonna have no problem with him, Bodie."

"You boys can just stay where you are while I go and have a talk with Mr. Gunsmith. Enjoy your drinks, boys. I'll be right back."

TWENTY-TWO

Miranda's disappearance still baffled Clint. If he had to, he didn't even think he could describe her. She'd been bundled up in a jacket, and all he was really able to tell was that she had a pretty face and great big eyes.

Where had she gotten to, and why?

With half a beer in his hand he turned to survey the setup of the saloon. At the same time he saw the big man coming toward him. He could tell from the way the man's chest was puffed out, and the way he was walking, that he was looking for trouble. He turned back to the bar.

"Lee, let me have a beer," the big man said.

"Comin' up, Bodie."

"How about you, Mr. Gunsmith?" Bodie asked. "You want another beer?"

"I'll just finish this one, thanks," Clint said.

"Hey," Bodie said, "whatsamatta? You too good to drink with me?"

Clint turned his head and looked into the man's face. He was about thirty, had a jaw like a slab of rock, and mean little eyes. He was the school bully, all grown up, who thought he could still throw his weight around.

"You're looking for trouble in the wrong place,

sonny," Clint said, deciding against trying to be nice. "Get lost."

At that moment, Lee arrived with Bodie's beer. He put it on the bar and sized up the situation quickly.

"Bodie," he said, "I don't want no trouble in here."

"Then you better tell Mr. Gunsmith here to mind his mouth," Bodie said. "He's talkin' pretty mean."

"Why don't you just leave him alone?" Lee asked.

Bodie looked at the barman and said, "When I want your opinion, bartender, I'll ask for it."

Then he turned back to Clint, backing up a few steps, letting his hand dangle down by his gun.

"I think you owe me an apology, Mr. Gunsmith."

Clint, still leaning on the bar, looked over his shoulder at the man and said, "Ain't going to happen, sonny."

"Well then, you and me, we got somethin' to settle."

At that moment, Lee brought his shotgun from beneath the bar and cocked both barrels.

"Not in my place, Bodie."

Bodie looked down the barrels of the shotgun.

"You're lookin' for trouble takin' a hand in this, Lee," he said. "It's none of your business."

"It is while you're in my place," Lee said. "I'm not lookin' for trouble, I'm lookin' to head it off."

Bodie looked from Clint to the bartender and back, flexing and unflexing his gun hand.

"You're gonna be sorry, Lee," Bodie said. He looked back at his two friends sitting at the table. "Come on, let's get out of here."

The two men grudgingly got up and followed their leader out of the saloon. Lee returned the shotgun to the shelf beneath the bar.

"Sorry you have to lose business because of me," Clint said.

"They'll be back," Lee said. "This is the only saloon in town."

"What's this Bodie's claim to fame?"

"He thinks he's a tough man because he's big and can pound people with his fists," Lee said. "He also fancies himself a hand with a gun."

"Is he?"

Lee shrugged.

"I've never seen him use it," the bartender said. "He usually gets his way by using his size."

Clint drained his beer mug, put the empty on the bar and said, "Thanks, Lee."

"You better be careful out there," Lee said. "I wouldn't put it past Bodie to wait for you."

"I'll be careful," Clint said. "I promised the sheriff I wouldn't shoot anybody while I'm here, but I guess that's going to be Bodie's decision."

"He won't face you alone," Lee said. "He'll have those other two backin' his play."

"That's the way it seems to go, lately," Clint said, shaking his head. "What happened to the days when a gunny wanted to face you all alone to make a name for himself?"

"Well, one thing is good."

"What's that?"

"Bodie didn't seem to be that drunk when he left," Lee said. "He might need a little more liquor before he tries you outside."

"Well, I guess there's only one way to find out," Clint said, and went through the batwing doors.

He paused outside so that his eyes could adjust to the darkness. He also stepped to the side so he wouldn't be backlit by the light coming from inside. When he could see well enough, he stepped down from the boardwalk and started across the street. He hoped he wasn't going to have to break his word to the sheriff—but then recalled that he'd said he didn't *intend* to shoot anyone.

Somehow, he doubted that this sheriff would see the difference.

TWENTY-THREE

Arnie Pace and his men were camped outside Deerfield. From where they were they could see the lights of the town.

"Looks like a good-size town, Arnie," Lowell said. "Why don't we take the bank while we're there?"

"Yeah," Roberts said, "make a little withdrawal."

"You can't hit a bank just like that," Pace said. "You got to go in and take a look at it and make a plan. The way you fellas want to do it, somebody's got to get killed."

"Well," Lowell said, "as long as it ain't one of us, what's the problem?"

Pax looked up at the sky as Arnie Pace turned to face Lowell and Roberts.

"We're passin' through that town to see if Jimmy Boy ended up there," he said, "and that's all. After that, we're on our way. I'm stickin' with my plan to get J. D. Land. Now, if you fellas want to hit that bank you're welcome to it . . . after Pax and I are gone. Got it?"

"Sure, we got it, Arnie," Lowell said.

"We don't want to hit no bank without you, Arnie," Roberts said.

"Well, then take your food and sit over there, away

from the fire. One of you is gonna have the first watch and one the second. Figure it out yourselves."

Lowell and Roberts picked up their plates and cups and moved away from the fire to eat and decide.

"What's on your mind, Arnie?" Pax asked.

"The kid was your nephew, Pax."

"Yeah, but we ain't that close."

"So if he turns up dead you ain't gonna go off half-cocked on me, are you?" Pace asked.

"Naw," Pax said. "Actually, I ain't even his real uncle. We're more like cousins. We ain't hardly related at all."

"Good," Pace said, "good. That means that even if he's dead I can continue to play J. D. until I get him."

"I'm with you on that all the way, Arnie," Pax said.

"Well," Pace said, "we'll have to keep an eye on those two idiots, then." He indicated Lowell and Roberts, who seemed to be in an argument over who was going to take what watch.

"Don't worry about them, Arnie," Pax said. "I'll talk to them."

"You know, years ago you rode with men you could trust," Pace said.

"Like Land?"

"Yeah, for a long time it was Land, and then he stabbed me in the back." Pace looked at Paxton and said, "Now, I just got you."

For a moment Pax didn't know how to take that, but then he decided that, in his own way, Pace had just paid him a compliment.

"I'll always be behind you, Arnie," Pax said. "We're partners."

"Sure, Pax," Pace said, "we're partners."

Arnie Pace continued to stare down at the lights of Deerfield as he finished his meal.

J. D. Land instinctively knew that his was the only camp in the area at that moment. The air didn't carry any telltale scents of anything downwind of him, and he was depending on his instincts as far as upwind went. Still, he knew he'd sleep lightly with his gun in his hand. The position had come back to him with such familiarity, even after being away from it for ten years.

He put on another pot of coffee so it would be there when he woke up, checked his Morgan, then checked the loads in his Colt. Satisfied that everything was as it should be, he wrapped himself in his blanket and tried to sleep.

Sleep was the one thing that had been eluding him since he started tracking Arnie Pace and his men. It was a lot easier to track five men than one, because they left behind a distinct trail of not only tracks, but cold campfires.

His sleep, though, was plagued by dreams, dreams of Miriam and Josh, lying dead, and then rising and approaching him with outstretched arms, demanding that he avenge them. He'd toss and turn and invariably would get up even before first light, just to escape the nightmares. Of course he was going to avenge them, so why did they have to haunt his dreams?

He hadn't given any thought to the vengeance he would take on God. He'd have to deal with that after his revenge on Arnie Pace and his men. He couldn't forget Pace's men. There had been too much violence done for one man. Arnie had been the leader, but his men had done a lot of the damage.

They would all pay.

Clint got back to his hotel without incident. Bodie and his friends had been nowhere to be seen.

Before going into the hotel he stood out front, took a deep breath and looked off into the hills. Suddenly, he saw the light and knew there was somebody up there, somebody camping. Why would they camp so close to town rather than come riding in? The only answer was that they wanted to ride in during the day. Someone who was tired from riding the trail didn't think like that. This had to be someone who planned what he wanted to do and did it in the daylight.

Tomorrow, he decided, might be an interesting day.

TWENTY-FOUR

Clint awoke the next morning thinking about the camp up on the hill. The men would probably break camp at first light and ride into town. He, on the other hand, was supposed to *leave* town with first light. The other possibility was that the men on the hill were there because they intended to bypass Deerfield. If they had enough supplies, there would be no need for them to stop.

He decided to go ahead and pack to leave, prepare his horse and then see what the morning brought.

Arnie Pace woke as Pax shook him.

"Arnie, time to get up."

"Coffee," Pace said, and Pax handed him a cup.

"We goin' into town?" Lowell asked.

Arnie sipped noisily at the hot coffee and then shook his head. "No, we ain't."

"What?" Pax asked.

"I decided that Lowell and Robby can go in and find out about Jimmy Boy. There's no reason we all have to go in."

"When did you decide that?" Pax asked.

"Just before I fell asleep." Pace, who didn't consider Pax a partner, even though the other man did, asked,

"Do you have a problem with that, Pax?"

"No, no problem," Pax said. "It just comes as a surprise is all."

"Hell, we don't mind goin' into town," Lowell said, "do we Robby?"

"Don't mind at all."

"Beer," Lowell said.

"Women," Robby said.

"A hot meal."

"A real bed."

"You ain't goin' on a vacation, boys," Pace said. "One day, one night, in and out. Find out what you can about Jimmy Boy and then leave."

"Right, Arnie," Lowell said.

"Right," Robby said.

Pace handed his empty cup to Pax and got to his feet.

"Have some coffee," he told the two men, "and then get goin'."

"No breakfast?" Robby asked.

"Get your breakfast in town," Pace said.

"I like that!" Lowell said. "Come on, Robby. Let's mount up."

As the two men went to their horses, Pax asked, "Why are you sendin' them in alone?"

"I want to keep movin'," Pace said. "I'm not where I want to be to face J. D. Land, and if we stop in town, he could catch up to us before I'm ready."

"Well, Arnie," Pax asked, "where do you want to be?"

"I don't know," Pace said, "but I'll know when I get there."

Clint took his gear to the livery, where he saddled Duke himself and then rode the big gelding to the front of the hotel. He decided to wait there until either the men from the camp came into town, or the sheriff came to chase him away—whichever came first.

TWENTY-FIVE

As the sheriff approached Clint a short time later, he could tell by the man's purposeful stride and demeanor what he had on his mind.

"It's started already," the lawman said.

"Good morning, Sheriff."

"I heard about the trouble last night, in the saloon."

"There was no trouble in the saloon, Sheriff."

"With Big Bodie?" Sheriff Townsend asked. "You don't remember that?"

"We talked," Clint said. "That's all I remember."

"Well . . . it could easily have become more than that," Townsend said.

"But cooler heads prevailed," Clint said. "I'm getting ready to leave town, Sheriff, as you can see."

Townsend looked at Duke, saddled and ready to go, and said, "I'm glad to hear it. Why don't you go now, before Bodie sobers up."

"I thought he had to be drunk to challenge me."

"Whether he's drunk or sober, I don't want any trouble."

"And neither do I," Clint said, "but I noticed something last night you should know about?"

"What's that?"

Clint told him about seeing the campfire.

"Where was that?" Townsend asked.

"Right up on that hill," Clint said, pointing.

"Could have been anybody."

"Yes, it could have," Clint agreed, "but if I'm not mistaken, you'll have some strangers riding into town fairly early this—oops."

Right down the street he saw two riders coming into town, riding slow, taking a look around.

"Wha—" Townsend said, and looked behind him.

"Wonder what they want?" Clint asked.

"It's my job to find out," Townsend said. "I'd appreciate it if you wouldn't interfere."

"The last thing I'd want to do, Sheriff," Clint said, "is interfere with your job."

"Glad to hear it. Just see that you don't."

Townsend turned and walked down the street to meet the two mounted men.

"It's the Sheriff," Roberts said, sounding panicky. "What do we do?"

"Relax," Lowell said. "We ain't done nothin' in this town."

"Oh, that's right."

"We're just lookin' for Jimmy Boy."

"Right."

They reigned in their horses and waited for the lawman to reach them. He didn't look like much, kinda short and pot-bellied, but they took the badge seriously.

"Mornin', Sheriff," Lowell said.

"Gents," Townsend said. "What brings you to town so early?"

"We're lookin' for a friend of ours who was supposed to be comin' this way," Lowell said.

"Oh? What's your friend's name?"

"Jimmy Boy—" Lowell started, but then stopped. "I mean, Jim Smith. We call him Jimmy Boy."

"A young fella?"

"That's right."

"You gents better get down from your horses," Townsend said. "I got some bad news for you."

Lowell and Roberts looked down at Jimmy Boy's body, which was lying on a table in the back room of the undertaker's.

Lowell looked at the sheriff.

"Who did you say killed him?"

"Clint Adams," Townsend said. "Do you know who he is?"

"We know," Lowell said.

"The Gunsmith," Roberts said, his tone touched with awe.

"That's right," the sheriff said, "so I hope you fellas ain't plannin' to do anythin' foolish."

"Foolish?" Roberts asked.

"Like goin' after Adams."

"Is he still in town?" Lowell asked.

Townsend mentally kicked himself for even mentioning it.

"Actually, he was just leaving this morning, when you two rode in," the sheriff said.

"Uh-huh," Lowell said. "Well, Sheriff, Jimmy Boy was a friend of ours, but not such a good friend that we'd try to go up against the Gunsmith. No, sir."

"That's good to hear. Do either of you gents want to pay to have him buried?" Townsend asked.

Lowell and Roberts exchanged a glance, then turned, said, "No," and walked out.

TWENTY-SIX

Clint watched as the two men left the undertaker's office, mounted up and rode out. Confused, he crossed the street and entered the office just as the sheriff was starting to leave.

"Did they know him?" he asked.

"Sure did."

"And they left? Didn't they want to bury him?"

"Nope," Townsend said. "Apparently, they weren't that close."

"So they just left?"

"Yep, and I wish you'd do the same. We'll toss this fella into an unmarked grave and everything will be back to normal around here."

"That's real important to you, isn't it?" Clint asked. "That everything be normal?"

"We don't like change around here too much."

"Well," Clint said, "I'm doing the right thing by leaving then."

"Yes, you are."

Actually, Clint wanted to leave and follow the trail of the two men who just left. If they were riding with Arnie Pace, they would lead him right to him. If they weren't . . . well, he wasn't wasting any more time following them than he was riding around aimlessly.

"Thanks for letting me visit your town, Sheriff."

"You're welcome."

"I wish I could say it was a nice little town."

"I wish I could say come back sometime."

There was nothing to say to that, so Clint left the undertaker's place, mounted up and rode out of town.

"What are we gonna tell Arnie?" Lowell asked.

"Never mind Arnie," Roberts said. "What do we tell Pax? The kid was his kin."

"We tell them the truth, then," Lowell said.

"Which is?"

"That somehow the kid got himself killed by the Gunsmith."

"All the truth?"

"Whataya mean?" Lowell asked.

"Do we say that we probably could have caught up to the Gunsmith if we tried?" Roberts asked.

"Why would we be dumb enough to try? You think they're gonna hold that against us?" He touched his temple. "It shows that we're smart—maybe smarter than either one of them thinks."

"If we're so smart," Roberts asked, "why are we going along with this vendetta Arnie has against his old partner?"

"Because when it's over," Lowell said, "Arnie will start picking jobs, and the money will be rolling in again."

"You know what I'm gonna do when that happens?"

"What?"

"Save," Roberts said.

"Save what?"

"Money, stupid."

"Why would you want to do that?"

"Well, it's better than spendin' it faster than we get it."

"I don't think so," Lowell said. "Money is for spendin'; otherwise, why the hell have it?"

"You can spend it on something other than whiskey and whores."

"What's better than that?"

Roberts shook his head and said, "I should know better than tryin' to talk to you. Just forget it."

"Jeez," Lowell muttered, "what's better than whores and whiskey?"

Clint's intention was to hold back and follow the trail the two men were leaving, but Duke was so much the better horse than either of theirs that he soon had them in sight. Now, instead of tracking them, he was following them.

Right to Arnie Pace—he hoped.

J. D. Land was grateful that he was trailing four men and not just Arnie Pace. He might not feel that way when he caught up to them, but the four men were leaving a clear trail behind them.

Maybe too damn clear.

It certainly occurred to him that this was all a trap, a ruse to get him where Arnie Pace wanted him, but he didn't see where he had much choice in the matter. After all, he wanted Pace at least as much as the man wanted him—and probably more. He had no choice but to continue to follow the trail, which he preferred to losing the damn thing for good.

He stopped from time to time in towns to gather a small amount of supplies, things he could simply carry on horseback. He never stayed in a town, though, never even stopped for a drink. Just a few supplies, and then he was on the trail once again.

Having been out of the saddle for so many years, it had taken days for his butt to become used to the saddle again, but it eventually happened. He had been riding free of pain and discomfort for quite a while.

When he crossed into Minnesota it suddenly felt colder to him. He'd heard people mention how cold a place it was, but now he could see that they were telling the truth. He'd spent most of his life in the southwest, but he knew that Arnie Pace came from Minnesota.

So Pace was heading for home, probably intending to face him there, which was just fine with J. D. Land.

Pace and Pax stopped in a town called Wellwood, deciding to spend the night off the trail.

"It'll give the boys a chance to catch up," Pace said.

"And not Land?"

"We're not gonna be here *that* long."

They left their horses in the livery and went to the hotel to get each of them a room.

"I'm gonna take a nap," Pace told Pax. "You keep an eye out for Lowell and Roberts."

"And Jimmy Boy."

Pace shook his head.

"Jimmy Boy's dead," he said, and went upstairs.

TWENTY-SEVEN

J. D. Land crouched and studied the remnants of the camp and then looked down the hill at the town of Deerfield. From what he could see, the four riders had split, two going around the town and two riding in. It looked like they had camped the night before and then split in the morning. He figured the camp was maybe a week old.

With no way to tell which pair had included Arnie Pace, he knew he was going to have to go into town and see what the story was there. Even if Pace had been in Deerfield, though, he doubted that the man would still be there. This was not where he'd hole up and wait to face him.

He stood straight up, walked to his horse, mounted and rode down to the town.

Sheriff Townsend looked up and frowned when he saw that the man who had entered his office was a stranger. Too many damn strangers had been in town already that week. Hopefully, this was the last.

"Help ya?"

"Yes, Sheriff," Land said, "I'm looking for a man named Arnie Pace."

"I know the name," Townsend said. "Why would one man be looking for Pace and his boys?"

"It's a private matter," Land said. "If you know the man can you tell me if he's been here within the past week?"

"Why do you ask about the week?"

"I found an old camp up in the hills—looks about a week old," Land said. "Like somebody was looking your town over from there."

"Well," the lawman said, sitting back in his chair, "we've had some strangers in here this week, but none of them was Arnie Pace."

"Are you sure?"

"Positive."

Land thought a moment, and while he did the lawman studied him. There was something familiar about this fella, but he couldn't quite place it.

"Who was here?"

"Hmm?" The question brought the sheriff back to the present. "What?"

"I asked you who was in town this week?"

"Well, a fella named Jim Smith was here, but he was dead."

"Dead?"

The sheriff nodded.

"Got killed on the trail, and another fella brought him."

"Anybody know him?"

"He had some letter on him gave us his name, but he wasn't really identified until these other two fellas rode in."

"And who were they?"

The man shrugged. "They didn't leave me their names."

"But they identified this Smith?"

The sheriff nodded. "They called him Jimmy Boy."

"Uh-huh. And did they stay in town to see to his burial?"

"Nope," the sheriff said, "they rode right out, which is what I'm hoping you do."

Land stiffened.

"Why would I want to do that, Sheriff."

"Because, Mister," Townsend said, sitting forward now, "you look like trouble to me, and I don't want trouble in my town."

"Did you tell that to the other strangers?"

"Didn't have to," the sheriff said. "They all left willingly."

"Well," Land said, "I wouldn't want to be the troublemaker, so I'll leave willingly, too."

"You look familiar to me," Townsend said. "Have we ever met before?"

"Not that I know of," Land said, honestly. "You're probably just familiar with the type."

"Maybe . . . but you're very familiar."

"I'll be on my way," Land said.

He walked to the door, but stopped before opening it.

"Something else?" Townsend asked.

"Yes, you said that another stranger had killed this Jimmy Boy Smith," Land said, "but you didn't say who it was."

"Didn't I?"

"No."

Townsend rubbed his jaw.

"Maybe you don't want to hear this."

"Maybe I should be the judge of what I do or don't want to hear," Land said, "Why don't you try me?"

"All right," Townsend said. "It was Clint Adams."

Land didn't say anything.

"You know, the Gunsmith?"

"I know who he is, Sheriff," Land said. "Thanks."

And he left the office.

TWENTY-EIGHT

Clint Adams was in Minnesota. Coincidence, Land wondered, or something else? What else could it be, though? Was he, too, trailing Arnie Pace, and if so, why? Did it have anything to do with what happened to Land's family?

Land, walking to his horse, assumed that the story of his family's murder must have made a few newspapers. Perhaps Clint Adams read the story, but they had only met once, for that one night. Why would Clint decide to take an active part in tracking down the killers?

No, his presence in Minnesota—and in Deerfield—must have been a coincidence. What he couldn't decide was whether it was a good thing or a bad thing.

He mounted his horse and rode out of town to once again pick up the trail of the Pace gang.

Clint was careful to give the two men enough of a lead on him so that they wouldn't feel like they were being followed, and so they wouldn't be able to see him if they turned for a look.

He knew he was expecting a lot for them to actually be Pace's men and lead him to the man, but he thought it was safe to assume that they were on the wrong side of the law. The young man he'd killed had certainly been a bad one, and he might have learned what he knew from these two—or from Arnie Pace.

He was surprised that the men rode on at a time when a traveler would normally be making camp. He assumed they knew of a town ahead that they could make before nightfall. He also knew if there *was* a town, he was going to have to camp outside for the night and enter come morning. If they were the men who had been camped on a hill outside Deerfield, they had switched places with him.

After a few more miles he saw the sign that announced the town of Wellwood up ahead. The population number had changed so many times that it was now blurred.

He followed them until they reached the main road and took it into town.

"What makes you think they stopped here?" Lowell asked Roberts.

"A hunch."

"Based on what?"

"Based on the fact that it's getting late and we didn't find a camp."

"Maybe they're camped on the other side of town."

"Let's just go with my hunch," Roberts said, "and see what happens, hmm?"

"Sure, Robby, sure," Lowell said. "No skin off my nose. Even if they're not here I can have a woman and a bed—not necessarily in that order.

Roberts smiled and said, "That's exactly what I'm thinkin'."

It was dusk when Pax saw the two riders coming in. When they saw him they looked as if they were disappointed, but then they waved and rode their horses over to where he was standing, in front of the hotel.

"This town got a whorehouse?" Lowell asked.

"I haven't checked," Pax said, "but that can be your job."

"Somebody's gotta do it."

"Put your horses in the livery around the corner, then come back here and check in. I'll let Arnie know you got here."

"Right," Lowell said.

"Don't you want to know what happened?" Roberts asked.

"Sure," Pax said, "but I can hear about it when you tell it to Arnie. Now go ahead."

"Pax, you might want to hear this now," Roberts said.

"All right, what?"

"Jimmy Boy is . . . dead."

Pax digested that news in silence, then said, "Get settled."

"See you in a few minutes," Roberts said.

As they rode away, Roberts asked, "What do you think of my hunch now?"

"Lucky," Lowell said, and laughed.

In point of fact, the town did have a whorehouse, because a short time after he'd decided to take a nap, Pace had come down and said to Pax, "Find me a whore."

"A whore? Where?"

"There's got to be a whorehouse in this town," the bandit leader said. "Get me one."

"Okay, Arnie, okay," Pax said. He went in search of a whorehouse, found one, went inside, looked over the girls, picked out one he knew Pace would like and paid the madam extra to have the girl go to Pace's room.

As they walked back to the hotel the girl said, "So I'm for somebody else?"

"That's right."

• • •

"Not for you?"

"Right again."

The girl was Arnie's type, not Pax's. Pax liked big girls, tall and full-bodied, while Arnie preferred short, petite girls. They didn't have to be well endowed, particularly, but Arnie liked a nice butt on a girl, and Pax thought he'd like this one.

"What's your name again?" Pax asked.

"Luisa."

Well, Luisa, my friend is gonna like you a lot."

"How come you're not gettin' a girl for yourself?" she asked.

"I don't have time. I have things to do."

"Cause I have this friend—Brenda? The redhead you saw? She can really do some things with—"

"That's okay," Pax said, "thanks. I'm not interested."

"Whatsamatter," she asked, playfully, "you don't like girls?"

He turned and looked at her and said, "I don't like dirty whores."

That shut her up, which suited him just fine.

Now Pax figured he was going to have to go upstairs and interrupt Pace during his pleasure taking. Of course, the girl might appreciate the interruption, because Arnie Pace was the type who liked to play rough. That was why he preferred tiny girls. He could knock them around real easy.

He went into the hotel with no thoughts for his dead relative, Jimmy Boy Smith. He went up the stairs to Arnie Pace's door and listened for a moment. He heard two different voices, both grunting—one probably in pleasure and the other in pain.

He knocked. The noises inside—voices, bedsprings—stopped, and footsteps came toward the door. When it opened, Arnie Pace glared out, his hair in wild disarray around his head. Behind him, Pax could see the little black-haired whore spread-eagled on the bed, on her stomach, her white buttocks showing red marks where Pace had probably used a belt on her.

"What?"

Pax backed away from Pace, both from his malevolent glare and from the fact that he was naked and aroused. His huge cock was glistening wet and pulsing.

"The boys are back," Pax said, "and they got news about Jimmy Boy."

"He's dead."

"Right."

Pace ran his hand over his hair in an attempt to smooth it down.

"That's not news."

"Maybe not, but I think they have something else to say."

"What?"

"They'll tell you."

"Okay, then," Pace said. "Tell them to get settled and meet us at the saloon in an hour."

At that point, the girl on the bed stirred and groaned, and it definitely wasn't a groan of pleasure.

Pace looked back over his shoulder as the girl began to move her legs. He stared at her bare ass, everything she had visible because her legs were splayed, and said to Pax, "Make that an hour and a half."

"Sure, Arnie."

"Go."

"Arnie?" Pax said, as Pace began to close the door.

"What?"

He wanted to say, "Don't kill this one," but he decided against it. In any case, Pace saved him the trouble.

"Don't worry, Pax," he said "I ain't gonna hurt her too much."

The door slammed in Pax's face.

• • •

As Pace approached the bed, he admired the red welts on the girl's ass. He'd just about done one of everything to her in the past few hours. In addition to the welts, she had bite marks on her thighs and little breasts, a split lip, and he'd fucked her so many times that her pussy had gone dry.

"Here we go, sweetie," he said. "No more interruptions."

He got behind her on the bed, gripped her hips and lifted her up onto all fours.

"Wait, wait . . ."she gasped. "W-wait a minute. . . ."

"Don't have time to wait or waste, darlin'," he said, spreading her cheeks so he could see her little brown hole.

"N-no," she said, "wait, you're dry, let me wet you. . . ."

"What are you gonna use for wet?" he asked. "Your cunt's dry, and you said your mouth hurt too much."

"No," she said, "I can lick you . . . I'll lick you and make you real wet . . . ." Her tone was desperate. She knew that if he invaded her from behind with no lubrication of any kind, it was going to be unbelievably painful.

"Now, remember," he said, leaning forward so he could whisper in her ear, "no screaming. You get paid double if you don't scream."

She knew that. That's why she had a split lip, because she'd bitten into it herself rather than scream.

"All right." She bit her lip again.

He spread the cheeks of her tiny, perfectly shaped ass, pressed the big, bulging head of his cock right up against her butthole, and pushed . . . .

TWENTY-NINE

Clint was careful to make his camp at a point where he would be able to see the town, but no one would be able to see his fire. He was also downwind of the town, so the smell of his camp would not drift that way.

There was, however, nothing to see. This town was slightly larger than Deerfield, but he wasn't close enough to actually see anyone. There were people walking up and down the street, but he didn't know if they were the men he had followed. Also, he was assuming that they had stopped in town and not just ridden through. If they were going to do that, they probably would have skirted the place.

He made sure Duke was taken care of before starting his fire and putting the coffee on. He was fairly certain that the two men had not noticed him following them. However, they may have found out from the sheriff or the undertaker that he was the one who had killed Jimmy Boy Smith. They would surely pass that information on to Arnie Pace. But he'd never met Pace, and neither of the two men had seen him, so he felt fairly safe riding into the town the next morning. He simply didn't want to ride in tonight, another stranger coming in right after two others arrived. He didn't want to attract any undue attention.

Of course, riding Duke was sort of hard since the big gelding was usually the target of such attention.

Arnie Price met his three men in the saloon after he was finished with the whore. He paid her the money and pushed her out of his room, barely giving her time to dress. She limped away, money held tightly in one small hand, and he wondered how much of that cash was really going to get to the madam.

As he entered the saloon he felt good. Sex always did that for him. He was happy, satisfied, energized and the best thing about it was he could play it back in his head at any time, every squeal of pleasure and groan of pain.

Pax, Lowell and Roberts were sitting at a table in the back. Pace got himself a beer from the bar and walked over to join them.

"Nice to see you boys back," Pace said.

Lowell and Roberts exchanged a glance. They both knew that the only time Arnie Pace was friendly was after he'd had sex and hurt some girl.

"What have you got tell me?" Pace asked.

"Uh, Jimmy Boy's dead," Lowell said.

"I know that," Pace said. "What else?"

"It was Clint Adams what killed him," Roberts said.

Pace touched the scar on his cheek thoughtfully.

"Where's Adams?"

"We don't know," Lowell said.

"Was he in town when you were?"

"No," Roberts said. "The sheriff there said he'd already left."

"You talked to the sheriff?"

"He braced us as soon as we rode into town."

"Sure he did," Pace said, "because he didn't want any trouble. Adams was still in town."

"The sheriff said he wasn't—" Lowell started.

"The sheriff was lying to you."

"Then . . . maybe he's still there," Lowell said.

"If he is, he can stay there," Pax remarked. "I don't want any part of the Gunsmith."

"And maybe he followed you here," Pace said.

The two men exchanged a glance again.

"I didn't see nobody," Lowell said.

"Me, neither," Roberts added.

"That don't matter," Pace said. "He could still have been there."

"And he might be here now," Pax said.

Lowell and Roberts looked around.

"I don't mean in here," Pax said, "I mean in town."

"Well, he could be in here," Lowell said. "After all, who knows what he looks like?"

"Never seen him," Pax said, "and I don't want to."

"Pax," Pace said, "we're leavin' town."

"Good," Lowell said. "I'll saddle the—"

"Not you," Pace said, cutting him off. "You and Robby are gonna stay here and take care of him."

"Take care of the Gunsmith?" Roberts asked. "Do you think we're crazy?"

"How hard is it to shoot somebody in the back?" Pace asked. "He can't hurt you if he don't see you comin'."

"Then why don't you do it?" Lowell asked.

"Because I've got enough to do to take care of J. D. Land, I don't need Clint Adams, too."

"But what if he kills us like he did Jimmy Boy?" Roberts asked.

"Then don't try to kill him," Pace said, "just keep him here a while."

"How?" Roberts asked.

"Figure it out," Pace said. "You've got brains, don't you?"

"But Arnie—"

"I'm warning you boys," Pace said. "If the Gunsmith interferes with my plans for J. D., I'll be comin' for you two, instead. Got it?''

''We got it,'' Roberts said.

''Pax,'' Pace said, ''let's get movin' now.''

''It's gonna be dark soon.''

''I know it, but we've still got some time to put some miles between us and this place.''

Pax, shaking his head, got up and headed for the door.

Pace pointed at the two men and said, ''Just stall him,'' and left.

Lowell looked at Roberts and said, ''We could get just as dead tryin' to stall him as tryin' to kill him.''

''Well, then,'' Roberts said, ''we might as well try to kill him.''

THIRTY

Clint rode early the next morning into Deerfield. It was actually too early for much activity, but the few people who were on the street stopped to look at Duke. The big gelding, though getting on in years now, was still an impressive sight. His black coat maintained the sheen of youth, and his massive neck held his head up high.

Clint took Duke to the livery, where he found the sixtyish liveryman grumbling to himself.

"Can I get some help?" he asked.

"Why?" the man said. "People around here been helpin' themselves. What do they need me for?"

"Well, I just got to town, and I'd like to leave my horse here."

"And when you gonna come and get 'im?" the man asked. "When I'm asleep?"

"Why would I do that?"

"I don't know why anybody would," the man replied, "but two fellers did just that last night."

"What did they do, exactly?"

"They came and got their horses and left town without paying what's owed me," the man said. "That's what they did."

"Did you know them?"

"Never saw them before they got here a couple of days ago."

It had to be Arnie Pace and one of his men. The two men Clint followed arrived only yesterday. He decided to double check.

"Two men rode in yesterday," he said. "Did they leave their horses here with you?"

"They did."

"Are those horses still here?"

"They are. Seems like we're attractin' a lot of strangers lately."

"And I'm one of them," Clint said, "but I think I'll only be here overnight."

"Well . . . will you pay in advance?"

"Sure."

That seemed to change the old man's mood as he pocketed the money and took Duke inside the stable after Clint removed his saddlebags and rifle from the saddle.

The only reason he could think of for Arnie Pace to sneak out of town without paying his livery bill is if he thought somebody was on his trail. He was going to have to find the two men he'd followed here and ask them a few questions.

As Clint rode by the hotel, both Roberts and Lowell were watching him. They waited until he'd gone past to come out onto the boardwalk.

"You know, there's somethin' we don't know," Lowell said.

"What's that?"

"What kind of law this town has," Lowell said. "What if we kill the Gunsmith and the sheriff comes a-runnin'?"

"We'll just tell him we killed the Gunsmith," Roberts said. "That's gonna make us pretty big men."

"Yeah," Lowell said, "you're right. So where should we do this?"

"He'll have to walk back from the livery," Roberts said. "Let's just wait for him to come around that corner, you on one side of the street and me on the other."

Lowell rubbed his hands together and said, "He'll never know what hit him."

Time and time again, Clint's life had been saved by an uncanny sixth sense that warned him of danger.

It was warning him now.

He stopped before following the turn the street made, heading back to town. Why would Pace leave two men behind instead of having them all leave at the same time? That was easy. He'd left two men behind to handle whoever was following him. Did he think it was J. D. Land? Probably not. Arnie Pace sounded like the kind of man who wanted Land to suffer. That was why he killed the man's family the way he had. So maybe he didn't know it was Clint Adams on his trail, but his men were probably going to try to take out the first stranger to ride in.

Clint wondered what kind of law Wellwood had.

Where was he? Lowell wondered. He looked across the street at Roberts, who shrugged and spread his hands. They'd been waiting too long already. What if Adams had left town already? There'd be hell to pay if they had to tell Arnie Pace that.

Lowell started to leave his hiding place in a doorway, but Roberts waved at him from across the street to stay. Apparently, his partner wanted to give Adams a little more time to complete his business at the livery.

He stepped back into the doorway. Roberts waved Lowell back into place. It wouldn't do to be too impatient. Any minute Clint Adams would come walking around that corner, with no idea of what was waiting for him.

Roberts had not chosen a doorway, but was hiding behind some crates that had been stacked in front of the hardware store. If he had decided to stay in a doorway he might not have heard the words that came to him that next moment.

"Just stand fast, friend," the voice said. "Act like nothing's wrong."

Roberts froze.

Clint decided to find another way into town from the livery. He circled around behind some buildings and came up an alley. From his vantage point he could see the man hiding behind the crates. Moments later he saw that man wave to another man who was in a doorway across the street. Obviously, they were waiting to ambush him, maybe even shoot him in the back.

He worked his way along the doorways on his side of the street, hoping that the man across the street would not spot him before he reached the man on this side. Finally, he was within spitting distance of the man behind the crates, and he removed his gun.

"Just stand fast, friend," he said. "Act like nothing's wrong."

He saw the man freeze.

"W-what's goin' on?" the man asked.

"That's my question," Clint said. "Why are you and your friend across the street waiting to ambush me?"

"W-what?" the man asked. "Mister, I don't even know who you are."

"Is that a fact?"

"It purely is."

"Well then, you're going to die ignorant," Clint said, and cocked the hammer on his gun, even though he didn't need to.

"Wait, wait, wait!" the man hissed. "Okay. You're Clint Adams, the Gunsmith."

"Very good," Clint said. "Now I'll ask another question, and you'll answer it, and we'll get along fine."

"O-okay."

"Do you ride with Arnie Pace?"

The man didn't answer.

"I'm only going to ask these questions once," Clint said.

"All right!" Roberts said. "Yeah, we ride with Pace."

"Is he in town?"

"No."

"When did he leave?"

"Last night."

"Why?"

"He figured you were on his trail."

"How did he figure that?" Clint asked.

Roberts told him about being in Deerfield—which Clint knew—and about everything they'd found out—which Clint didn't know. Now, it seemed obvious that Pace was not only brutal and dangerous, but smart, as well. This was a good thing to know about your opponent when you were tracking him.

"So he left you and your friend over there to kill me?"

"Stall," Roberts said. "He left us to stall you."

"And you were going to do that by killing me?"

"No, no, we were gonna, uh—"

"Bushwack me."

"No, no really—"

"Call your friend over here and do it nice and casual."

"W-what are you gonna do?" Roberts asked. "Are you gonna kill us?"

"No," Clint said, "I'm going to stall you."

THIRTY-ONE

"Take your gun out left-handed and drop it on the ground."

Roberts did as he was told.

"Now kick it toward me."

The man obeyed.

"Now wave your friend over."

Roberts stood and waved to the man across the street. Lowell stepped from his doorway to peer over at Roberts, to make sure he was seeing right. Once again, Roberts waved. Finally, Lowell stepped into the street and started across.

"We can do this real easy," Clint said. "I'll take his gun and march the two of you over to the sheriff."

"We—we ain't done nothin' in this town."

"Only because I stopped you from trying to bushwack me."

"I tol' you we didn't—"

"Save it for the sheriff," Clint said. "Besides, as soon as I tell him you're with the Pace gang he'll be very happy. I'm sure there are rewards out on you, and I'm not going to claim it. Yes, I think I'm going to make the sheriff of Wellwood a very happy man, today."

"They'll hang us," Roberts said.

"Maybe."

"No, they will!" Roberts said, starting to blubber. "We're wanted dead or alive for murder. They'll hang us!"

"Get a good lawyer."

"What's the difference," Roberts asked, "if you kill us now or they hang us later?"

This was going in the wrong direction, but before Clint could think of a way to redirect it, Roberts made a move.

"Lowell! It's him! It's the Gunsmith!"

He tried to leap over the crates he was hiding behind, but they were empty and crumbled beneath his weight.

Lowell stopped, more than halfway across the street, and went for his gun. Clint had no choice. He stepped from cover and shot the man in the chest. Lowell went over backward, sprawled dead in the dirt, his gun still in his holster.

Roberts extricated himself from the shattered cartons and ran into the street. He was going for Lowell's gun.

"Stop!"

Roberts kept going. He reached Lowell and fell to his knees next to him. Before he could pluck the man's gun from his holster Clint fired into the dirt right near him. Roberts froze and looked up at Clint with wide eyes.

"This is a mistake," Clint said. "You already got your friend killed, why join him?"

"I tol' you," Roberts said. "I don't wanna hang."

"Maybe we can make a deal."

"What kind of deal? Will you let me go?"

"No," Clint said. "I'll still turn you over to the law, but I won't tell him that you're part of Arnie Pace's gang."

"What good will that do?"

"He'll probably hold you for a few days and then let you go. That's all the head start I need."

"What do I have to do?"

"Simple," Clint said. "Tell me where Arnie Pace is going."

"See? See?" Roberts said. "It's not fair. I'm dead, again. When Arnie finds out what I—"

"He won't find out," Clint assured the man. "He won't find out from me, and when I catch up to him, he won't be able to kill anyone."

"I—I don't know for sure where he's going."

"Is he luring J. D. Land up here to Minnesota?"

Roberts looked surprised, but said, "Yes."

"Why did he kill Land's family?"

"Revenge," Roberts said. "Arnie wants to hurt the man bad before he finally kills him."

"Why? Land has been out of it for ten years. Why now?"

"Arnie's real patient," Roberts said. "He wanted Land to get real happy and comfortable, so it would hurt more when Arnie took it all away."

"So he must be leading Land someplace that means something to one of them," Clint said aloud.

"Well . . ."

"Well what?"

"Arnie was born in Minnesota."

"What town?"

"I ain't sure, but it's north."

"How many men are with Pace now?"

"Just one," Roberts said. "Paxton Lewis. Everybody calls him Pax."

"So it's just the two of them?"

"For now," Roberts said. "They expect us to catch up to them."

Clint turned and saw from the corner of his eye a man wearing a badge approaching them.

"Here comes the law, Roberts," Clint said. "If Arnie wants you to catch up, it means you know where he's going."

"North. Just north. I swear! We were just supposed to follow his trail."

"The trail he's been leaving for Land to follow, right?"

"Right."

"What's going on here?" the sheriff shouted. He had his hand on his gun but had not drawn it. He looked experienced—in his forties—and also had the look of a man who would use his gun when he drew it.

"Sheriff," Clint said, turning to face the man, "my name is Clint Adams, and I have a story—"

At that moment Roberts saw his chance. He grabbed Lowell's gun and drew it out of the holster. Clint heard the sound of metal on leather, turned and fired once. The bullet struck Roberts in the chest and exploded in his heart. He fell dead across the body of his partner.

"Mister," the sheriff said, looking at the two bodies, "you got one *helluva* lot of explainin' to do."

THIRTY-TWO

Clint had to give up his gun and accompany the sheriff to his office while several townsmen and a deputy removed the bodies from the street.

In his office, the sheriff listened to Clint's story with great interest. Clint's gun was sitting on the desk next to the man's arm.

"That's a very interesting story, Mr. Adams," Sheriff Clyde Martin said when Clint finished. "My problem is, I have no one to back up your story."

"Try the liveryman," Clint said. "He'll tell you I just rode in and was asking about some men."

"That still doesn't tell me that these two men tried to ambush you, or that they actually do ride with Arnie Pace."

"Look, Sheriff, you know who I am," Clint said. "Have you ever heard that I killed people for no reason?"

"Well, no."

The one thing Clint didn't tell the sheriff about was J. D. Land. Clint was hoping that after Land had his revenge, he'd want to once again fade into obscurity. The fewer people who knew that he was back, the better it would be for him.

"Look, I'm tracking Arnie Pace. These two men were lying in wait for me when I got here."

"How did you know that?"

"I felt it. My guess is you've been a lawman for a long time. You must know that feeling."

"Well, yes, I do."

"I got the drop on them, but they were foolish. You saw the second man go for the fallen man's gun. It was an act of desperation. I *told* him I was simply going to hand him over to you, but he preferred to try for the gun. It was his choice."

The sheriff drummed his fingers on the desktop right next to Clint's gun. In the end, he grabbed the gun and handed it across to Clint.

"I'll have to verify that they were part of the Pace gang before you get any reward," he said.

Clint holstered his gun and said, "I don't want a reward, Sheriff. You can have that."

The sheriff shook his head.

"I don't get a reward for doing my job."

"Okay, then," Clint said, standing, "give it to the town. I'm sure the town council could put it to good use."

The sheriff thought a moment and then said, "Okay, I can do that. When will you be leaving?"

"Don't worry," Clint said. "I'm going to walk out of here and leave. I don't want any more trouble."

"That's good to hear."

The sheriff stood up but did not offer Clint his hand.

"Good luck with your hunt," he said. "Arnie Pace is a bad one. Oh, and he's got a guy named Lewis at his right hand. Also a dangerous man."

"Okay, thanks," Clint said. "I'll bear that in mind."

Clint made for the door but before he could go through it the sheriff called out to him.

"You might find this helpful," the man said.

''What's that?'' Clint asked, with the doorknob in his hand.

''Arnie Pace?'' the sheriff said. ''He's a local boy.''

''Born here?''

''No, but born in Minnesota.''

''Would you happen to know where?''

''As it happens,'' the sheriff said, ''I do.''

THIRTY-THREE

Paxton Lewis stared across the campfire at Arnie Pace, who seemed lost in thought. Pax knew the look. Arnie was replaying in his mind a time when he had hurt somebody. Maybe it was the girl in Wellwood, maybe it was J. D. Land's wife and kid. There was no way to know for sure, but the man had *that* look on his face.

"Arnie?"

No answer.

"Arnie?"

This time Pace acted startled, as if he'd forgotten that Paxton Lewis was even there.

"What is it?"

"I think we have to face somethin'."

"What?"

"It's been days since we left Lowell and Roberts."

"So?"

"So . . . they probably botched their job and ended up getting killed by the Gunsmith."

"Again, so?"

"It's down to just the two of us," Paxton said, "against J. D. Land and the Gunsmith."

"All right," Pace said, "which one do you want?"

"On second thought," Pace said, "you get the Gunsmith, because I'm not giving Land up. He's mine."

"Did you hear what I said? It's just the two of us now, Arnie."

"Against two of them," Pace added. "That sounds pretty even to me."

"But they're J. D. Land and the goddamned Gunsmith!"

Pace bristled.

"Are you sayin' you don't think I can handle J. D. Land? He's a goddamned preacher, for Chrissakes."

Pax knew better than to tell Arnie Pace he couldn't handle somebody, so he backed off.

"All I'm sayin' is I don't know if I can handle the Gunsmith."

"Well," Pace said, "we can deal with that problem, Pax."

"How?"

"First, I doubt that the Gunsmith and J. D. are gonna catch up to us at the same time. We'll probably have to deal with one, and then the other."

"And second?"

"Second," Pace said, "in a day or two I'll be home, where I have friends who will be only too glad to back us up. So you see? You're worrying for no reason."

"I think havin' the Gunsmith after you is reason enough."

"What? No fear of J. D. Land?"

"He was J. D. Land a long time ago," Pax said. "Like you said, he's just a preacher now."

"Oh," Pace said, happily, "I'll bet he's an ex-preacher by now."

J. D. Land rode into Wellwood several days after Clint Adams had left. A quick look at the hotel register told him that Clint Adams had not stopped there. He did not see Arnie Pace's name, either, and wondered if the man had registered under another name.

He did, however, talk with the sheriff, who told him about the two men Clint Adams had killed.

"Who were they?" he asked.

"Well, Adams claimed they rode with Arnie Pace."

"What did you tell him?"

"I told him I didn't know, but since then I've verified it. Their names were Lowell and Roberts, and then did ride with him."

"How about a Jimmy Smith?"

"Yep, that name came up, too."

So, Clint Adams was ahead of him and seemed to be doing his job for him. He had to reach Arnie before Clint did, though.

"What else did you tell Clint Adams, Sheriff?"

The lawman's eyes narrowed.

"Why are you so interested?"

"Because I think Adams and I are after the same man."

"You after the reward?"

"No," Land said, "I don't want any reward."

"That's what Adams said. He also said the town could keep the reward," the sheriff said.

"All right," Land said, "when I take Arnie Pace, this town can have the full reward amount."

Land didn't care if the town got it, or if this was the sheriff's way of putting his hands on it. It didn't matter to him who got the reward money, as long as he got Arnie Pace.

"So what did you tell him, Sheriff?"

"I told him," the lawman said, "where Arnie Pace was born."

THIRTY-FOUR

Arnie Pace had been born in a town called Grand Forks, Minnesota. It was right on the border of Minnesota and the Dakotas, and about seventy-five miles south of the Canadian border.

As they rode into Grand Forks, Pax noticed that it was considerably colder here than the rest of Minnesota, and he mentioned it.

"Got cold air comin' down from Canada way," Arnie Pace said. "Don't it feel great?"

"If you like the cold so much," Pax asked, "why did you spend so much time in the Southwest?"

"Because that's where I do my business," Pace said. "This is where I come to relax."

"So why lead J. D. here?"

Pace smiled.

"I want to be nice and relaxed when I kill him."

They went to one of Grand Forks' hotels to check in.

"Don't you have a house here or somethin'?" Pax asked.

"Used to," Pace said. "My parents' house, really, but it's gone. Burned to the ground. I just stay here when I come back home. They give me a real decent price."

They entered the hotel, which had a cozy, warm lobby. The desk clerk looked up to see who his visitors were and smiled when he saw Pace.

"Arnie!" he shouted. "Goddamn, boy, it's good to see you."

The man, the same age as Pace, came around the desk and rushed the other man. He crushed Pace in a bear hug, lifting him off his feet. He could do that because he was the biggest man Pax had ever seen.

"Put me down, ya bastard! You're gonna break me."

The man put Pace down and backed off to take a look at him.

"Paxton Lewis, this is Bear Morgan."

"Bear?"

"Real name's Stuart," Pace said, "but if you call him that he'll hurt you—won't you, big fella?"

"I don't hurt people," Bear said. He held out a huge paw to Pax. "Good to meet you."

"Yeah, likewise." Pax expected a bone crushing grip from the big man and was surprised when he didn't get one.

"What brings you back?" Bear asked Pace.

"I miss home."

"Then you should come back permanently."

"It's somethin' to think about," Pace said. "You got a room for us?"

"A room each? Sure. Right this way."

He walked them to the desk where he gave them each a room key without bothering to register them.

"Won't the owner get mad if we don't sign in?" Pax asked.

"He might," Bear said, "but since I am the owner, I don't think it's gonna be a problem. Why don't you two get settled in your rooms. I'll get somebody to mind the store and we can go get a drink."

''Sounds good, Bear,'' Pace said. ''We'll be down in about fifteen minutes.''

''Damn, it's good to see you, Arnie.''

''Good to see you, too, Bear.''

To Pax's surprise, Arnie Pace apparently meant it.

THIRTY-FIVE

Paxton Lewis had never seen this side of Arnie Pace. When they went to the saloon with Bear Morgan, there were at least half a dozen more bear hugs put on Pace, though none as powerful as Bear's.

Pax didn't know that Pace actually had *friends.* He'd once thought of himself as Pace's only friend, and as his partner, but lately he was starting to see that he was neither of those things. Pace had his own circle of friends; he simply kept them at Grand Forks. But did these men have any idea who Arnie Pace was to the rest of the world, when he left Grand Forks?

Pax drank free as Pace's friends kept buying them drinks, but he wasn't happy. He felt left out. Suddenly, he was the man he had always felt Arnie Pace was—the man with no friends.

What he had to do was get Pace out of Grand Forks, and the sooner, the better.

Clint was camped and was cooking up some bacon and beans when he became aware that someone was out in the darkness. He waited, tense and alert, for somebody to make a move, but in the end it was simply a voice that came from the dark.

"Hello, the camp!"

A woman's voice.

"I'd like to come in, if you don't mind."

"Come ahead," Clint called back.

When she entered the circle of light from his fire, leading her horse, he saw that it was Miranda—if that was even her name.

"Well, well," Clint said, "the disappearing lady."

"That bacon and beans smell good," she said. "So does the coffee."

"I'd offer you some," Clint said, "but I'm afraid you'd eat and run."

She made a face and said, "I guess I deserve that—but I really am hungry. I haven't had any time or money to buy supplies."

Clint stared at her a few moments, then said, "All right. Put your horse with mine, and then you can have some."

"Thank you."

"But you owe me an explanation."

"I'll give you one."

"Okay."

Miranda walked her horse to where Duke was, unsaddled it, saw to it and then returned to the fire. By that time Clint had a plate of bacon and beans and a cup of coffee to hand her. She took it and sat down across the fire from him. He helped himself, and they started to eat.

"You know," he said, "without you to back me up, I had to convince the law all by myself that I killed that man in self-defense."

"I know," she said, "I'm sorry, but I had to go."

"Why?"

Around a mouthful of bacon and beans she said, "I can't let him get too far ahead of me."

"Who?"

"The man I'm tracking."

"And who would that be?"

"You don't know him," she said. "His name's Arnie Pace."

"Oh, I know him."

"You do?"

Clint nodded.

"In fact, I'm tracking him, too."

She stopped eating and stared at him.

"Are you gonna kill him?"

"I don't know."

"Cause if you are, you're gonna have to kill me first."

"You're tracking him to defend him?"

"No," she said, "I want to kill him myself."

"What did he do to you?"

"Not to me," she said, "to my sister."

"And what was that?"

"He killed her." She put the plate down on the ground, as if she'd suddenly lost her appetite.

"I'm sorry," Clint said, "How did it happen?"

"My sister was no saint—she was whore—but she didn't deserve what he did to her," Miranda said. "You see, Arnie likes to hurt women while he's having sex with them. Most of the ones he hurts are lucky enough to walk away and recover, and he does pay them well, but—"

"Your sister wasn't one of the lucky ones, huh?"

"No."

"Where did this happen?"

"A small, nothin' town in Wisconsin."

"When?"

"Months ago."

"And you're still tracking him?"

"Well, tracking's not the right word, I guess," she said. "I'm no tracker. I'm just lookin' for him. I heard that he was born in Minnesota, so I guess I just keep waitin' for him to come back. Every once in a while I widen my search area, but I always end up back here—and I hate it here. It's too damn cold!''

Clint didn't wonder. She was wearing a pair of jeans and a poncho, but he didn't know what was underneath the poncho. What she needed was a fur-lined jacket, like the one he was wearing.

''Yeah, it is cold.''

She finished her coffee and he asked, ''Some more?''

''Thanks.''

''Are you armed?'' he asked, refilling her cup.

''I have a rifle.''

''Know how to use it?''

''Yes.''

''You'd probably do better with a handgun, though,'' Clint said. ''You could get closer.''

''I don't care how far or close I am to him,'' she said. ''I'm gonna kill him for what he did to my sister.''

Obviously, she was not giving Clint the whole story. Even if there had been a sister, Pace had obviously also done something to her.

''You know what Arnie looks like?'' he asked.

''Yeah, why?''

''Because I know where he's headed,'' Clint said. ''At least, I know where he was born.''

''You do? Take me, you gotta take me!''

''That's what I was thinking,'' Clint said. ''I don't know what he looks like.''

''You can take a good look at his body, after I finish with him,'' she said.

''Miranda,'' he said, ''we can do this together, but first we're going to have to come up with some rules.

THIRTY-SIX

They rode together all the next day, discussing the "rules" that Clint wanted to set forth between them.

Miranda was in favor of no rules—or rather, just one, which she made known when they stopped to rest the horses in the afternoon.

"The first one who finds him gets him."

"Do you really think you can take a man like Arnie Pace?" he asked her.

"I just need to get him in my sights."

"Ah," Clint said, "maybe even from the back?"

She gave him an angry look.

"And why not? Does he deserve better?"

"It's not him I'm worried about," Clint said. "If you shoot him down in cold blood, it's you I'm worried about."

"No jury would convict me."

"Have you ever killed a man before?"

"No."

"It's not an easy thing to do," he said, "but doing it is easier than trying to live with it afterward."

"You've killed many men."

"And I see all their faces, at one time or another, in my dreams."

"But why? I mean, you're the Gunsmith . . . your reputation . . ."

"You think because of who I am that killing a man means nothing to me?" he asked. "You don't know anything about me, Miranda, and I know even less about you."

"Meaning?"

"Meaning I think there is more at stake here than avenging your sister. What else happened between you and Pace?"

She stood up from the rock she'd been sitting on, her back stiff.

"I think we should split up here, Mr. Adams. I thank you for sharing your camp with me last night."

"Miranda—"

"I'll ride ahead, if you don't mind," she said. Please don't try to catch up. We'll be more noticeable together than we would be apart.

He had to give her that.

He watched her mount up and ride out, and he made himself comfortable for a few more minutes.

It was actually twenty minutes later when he decided to rise and remount his horse. Before he could do so, however . . .

"I was wondering if I would catch up to you," a voice said. "The sheriff back in Wellwood told me of a short cut."

Clint turned and looked not at Reverend Land, but at J. D. Land, dressed in black and wearing a holster, which looked very natural to him. In fact, this man even stood differently from the man he had met in Peculiar.

"That was a very lovely girl," Land said. "What did you do to her to drive her away?"

"It's not what I did to drive her away," Clint said. "It's what Arnie Pace did to drive her on."

"Ah," Land said, "another of Arnie's victims."

"I'm afraid so."

"What did he do to her?"

"All she'll admit is that he killed her sister," Clint said, "but I'm sure there's more."

"That sounds like enough to me."

"I'm sorry about your family, Rev—I mean—"

"J. D. will do," Land said, "and thank you."

"Can I ask you something personal?"

"Sure, why not?"

"What was it like to put the gun back on after so many years?"

Land looked down at the gun he wore on his hip, then he looked back at Clint.

"Unfortunately," he said, "it was as if I'd never taken it off."

Clint nodded, understanding.

"Are you in a hurry to get going?" said Land.

"Not if you know a shortcut to Grand Forks."

"I do. Is that where the girl is headed?"

"I'm afraid so," Clint said. "I, uh, told her where Arnie was born."

"Why did you do that?"

"I thought we were going to ride together," Clint said, "but she preferred to go it alone."

"It doesn't matter," Land said. "We'll get there well ahead of her. We have some time to talk."

"All right," Clint said, "let's talk."

Land was interested in Clint's reason for joining the chase. After Clint explained, Land stared at him.

"You met me and my family once and that was enough for you to do this?" he asked.

"It seemed like a good reason."

"And how many of Arnie's men have you killed?"

"Three."

"That leaves him and . . ."

"A man named Paxton Lewis—but we do have to

remember that we're going to Arnie's home town. He'll probably have lots of help there."

"It won't matter how much help he has," J. D. Land said, "as long as I can get to him."

"J. D., I think we have a different agenda here."

"What do you mean?"

"Well, I'm after Arnie, we have that in common," Clint explained, "but I would like to come out of this alive. I don't think you have the same intention."

"I don't intend to die, Clint," Land said, "but I'm willing to in order to exact my revenge. If you can't deal with that, then I might have to take my shortcut all alone. By the time you get to Grand Forks, it'll all be over."

"If he's there."

"He'll be there," Land said. "Arnie never told me where he was born—or if he did, I forgot—but he did always talk about home. That's where he'll want to stop and take me on."

"There's no need for us to split up now that we've joined forces," Clint said. "It's just important that we each know what the other's intentions are."

"Agreed."

"Well then," Clint said, "your shortcut."

They mounted their horses.

"Follow me," Land said. "It should be less than a day's ride from here."

"That would put us there in the dark. What about the girl?"

"She'll have to camp and won't get there until tomorrow afternoon," Land said. "By that time we'll be finished with Arnie."

"Good," Clint said, "she might actually get there in time to bury us."

Miranda, however, had changed her mind soon after leaving Clint and had ridden back to tell him. When she saw the two men talking, she knew that the other one was the man he'd told her about, whose family Arnie Pace had killed. She stayed out of sight, and when they left, she decided to follow them.

THIRTY-SEVEN

"Somebody's behind us," Clint said.

"Who is it?' Land asked. He was well out of practice to have detected this himself.

"I don't know," Clint said, "but it's one rider."

"What should we do?"

"First bend we come to you keep going," Clint said. "I'll double back and find out who it is."

"All right."

Eventually they came to that bend and as Land kept going, Clint peeled off to ride in a circle and come up behind the person following them. When he spoke from behind her he startled her.

"I thought you were going off on your own."

She whirled in her saddle, eyes wide with surprise, but relaxed when she saw it was him.

"I changed my mind and came back to tell you, but I saw the other man with you. Is that Land?"

"That's him."

"And now you two are riding together?"

"He's the reason I'm here," Clint said, "him and his family. Plus, he knows a shortcut to Grand Forks."

"That's handy."

"Why don't we go and tell him who was following

us?'' Clint suggested. ''I know he'd like to meet you.''

He rode up alongside of her and together they trotted up to join J. D. Land.

Land thought briefly of riding off and leaving Clint behind, but decided against it. He was right about one thing. In Arnie's hometown he would have a lot of friends and a lot of help. Clint would be useful to have around as a backup.

When he heard the sound of two riders behind him, he turned his horse and waited for them to reach him.

''Ah,'' he said, as he saw that the other person was a woman. ''Is this the lovely lady we were talking about? Miranda?''

''This is her,'' Clint said. ''Miranda, meet J. D. Land.''

''Mr. Land,'' she said. ''I'm very sorry for what happened to your family. I sympathize with you.''

''Well,'' Land said, ''from what Clint tells me, I believe that you do. I'm also sorry about your sister.''

''Thank you.''

''Well,'' Clint said, ''here we are.''

''Shall we travel as a threesome?'' Land asked.

''We each have our own goals in mind,'' Clint said.

''We don't have to think alike to ride together,'' Miranda said.

''The lady has a point,'' Land said, ''don't you think?''

''Unfortunately,'' Clint said, ''I do.''

''Well, then,'' Land said, ''since I know the shortcut, I'll take the lead.''

''Lead on,'' Clint said, and he and Miranda fell in behind him.

THIRTY-EIGHT

They rode together until nightfall.

"I thought you said this shortcut would get us there tonight," Miranda complained when they decided to camp.

"It probably would," Land said, "but we need to get the lay of the town before we do anything, and we can't do that in the dark."

"He's right," Clint said. "Even if we could see the lights of the town from here, we'd have to camp."

"What if I rode in alone?" she asked.

"First of all," Clint said, "a woman riding into town at night, alone, would attract attention."

"Secondly," Land said, "am I mistaken in assuming that Arnie knows you on sight?"

She sighed and said, "Yes, he does."

"So we'll all wait to ride in tomorrow."

"Won't that attract attention?" she asked. "All of us riding in together—and Arnie knows you by sight, too, doesn't he, Reverend?"

Land bristled.

"Don't call me that!"

His response startled Miranda.

"I'm sorry," she said, "I didn't mean anything by it."

"I . . . just don't have the right to be called that anymore," Land said.

"Have you stopped believing in God?" she asked.

He didn't answer right away.

"Because I have," she said. "If I still believed, then I'd leave Arnie to God's vengeance, but since I don't . . ."

"You know," Land said, not looking at Clint, "I asked a man once if he believed in God."

"Once?"

"His was the most interesting answer I ever heard," Land said.

"What was it?"

"He said that if God existed he had a lot of explaining to do."

Only then did Land look at Clint, who did not respond.

"I like that," Miranda said, "I like that a lot."

Clint cooked more of the same food he'd been eating on the trail—bacon and beans.

"Same thing for breakfast and supper?" Miranda teased. "Can you cook anything else?"

"Actually," Clint said, "no. I'd be totally lost in a real kitchen. What about you?"

"Oh, I can cook," she said, "but I'm better in a kitchen than on the trail. That's one thing I've discovered about myself since I hit the trail."

"And when was that?" Land asked.

"Months ago."

"And before that?"

She hesitated, then said, "Well, before that I'd never been on the trail."

"And you've come this far, inexperienced?" Land asked. "I admire you for that, Miss . . ."

''Just Miranda,'' she said.

''All right, Miss Just Miranda,'' Land said. This was the closest he'd come to telling a joke since the death of his family. ''You can call me J. D.''

They split up their duties so that Land took care of the horses, Miranda collected firewood and Clint made the fire and cooked.

When Land returned to the fire, he said, ''That gelding of yours almost took my hand off.''

''Oh, sorry,'' Clint said. ''I guess I should have warned you about him. He's not to keen on strangers.''

''Obviously not.''

''I smell bacon and beans,'' Miranda said, coming up on them.

Clint looked over his shoulder at her.

''You don't have to eat any if you don't want to.''

''I love bacon and beans,'' she said, ''and I'm hungry enough to eat a horse.''

Duke snorted as she said this, and her eyebrows went up.

''He understands?''

''Sometimes I think he understands everything,'' Clint said, handing her a full plate. He filled another and gave it to Land, and then made one for himself. That done, he poured out three cups of coffee and passed them around.

''All right,'' Miranda said, ''what do we do tomorrow?''

Clint and Land looked at each other.

''Someone must have a suggestion,'' she said.

''Well . . .'' Clint said.

''Go ahead,'' Land said. ''Let's hear it.''

''I'm the only one Arnie won't recognize.'' Clint said. ''Therefore, I was thinking I should go in first and get the lay of the town.''

''You wouldn't just be trying to get a shot at the reward, would you?'' Miranda asked.

"I don't think we have to worry about that," Land said before Clint could answer. "The sheriff back in Wellwood already told me that Clint promised the reward to the town."

"Did you make the same deal?" Clint asked.

"I had to," Land said, "in order to get the shortcut."

"Well, that's fine with me," Miranda said, "because I'm not in this for the reward, either."

"Then we're agreed?" Clint asked.

"We're agreed that you go in first," Land said, looking at Miranda, who nodded. "That makes sense, but what happens after that?"

"I'll come back here and let you know what I've found. It shouldn't take me more than an hour to locate him."

"And what if you're not back in an hour?" Miranda asked.

"Well, then," Clint said, "you two can come in with guns blazing."

They looked like they both liked that idea.

They decided to keep on watch overnight, since they were so close to town. When they split it, Clint came up with the first watch, since he was going to be riding into town early.

He was sitting in front of the fire, stoking it without looking into it, when Miranda appeared on the other side.

"I thought you were asleep."

"I can't sleep," she said. "Mind if I sit with you?"

"Not at all."

"Or I could take your watch, and you can take mine," she offered.

"That's okay," he told her. "I'm not sleepy, either."

"Is there coffee left?"

"I made a pot for my watch," he said and poured her a cup and one for himself.

"I was wondering," she said, "what you—both of you—must think of me?"

"Why?"

"Well, I haven't been acting very ladylike."

"As long as you feel what you're doing is right," Clint said, "why should you care what we—or anyone—thinks?"

"I just—well, I wouldn't want . . . I just do care, I guess, since we're out here together."

"Well, I don't think badly of you, Miranda," Clint said, "and I'm sure J. D. doesn't either."

"That's good."

"But . . ."

"But what?"

"I'm sure when the right time comes you'll tell us the truth about what's driving you."

"I told you, Arnie Pace killed my sister."

"Well," Clint said, "that's sure reason enough, but I can't help feeling there might be more to it than that. If I'm wrong, I apologize."

She finished her coffee and handed him the empty cup.

"I think I'll try to get some sleep now," she said.

"I'm sorry," he said, "I didn't mean to pry."

"That's all right," she said. "I believe . . . everything will come out . . . in the end."

Clint watched Miranda walk back to her bedroll and thought to himself, *I sure hope so.*

THIRTY-NINE

Clint woke the next morning feeling refreshed and alert. It was a relief to know that there was some definite purpose ahead of him, and he didn't just have to ride the trail in search of some sign. Grand Forks was ahead, and the end of this ordeal—more an ordeal for Land and Miranda than him—would soon be over.

Land had awakened him with a cup of coffee, holding one himself.

"She's still asleep," Land said.

Clint looked over at Miranda, wrapped in her blanket. The cup of coffee was warming his hands very nicely.

"Let her sleep," he said. "I'll be back in a little while."

"You better be real careful who you talk to, Clint," Land said.

"I was thinking that," Clint said. "I was wondering if it would be smarter to go into town in the afternoon, when the saloon was open."

"A bartender could probably tell you what you want to know, but then a lot of Arnie's friends would be up and around."

"I thought of that, too," Clint said. "I'm wondering if he counts the sheriff among his friends."

Land frowned.

"That wouldn't be good," he said, "but he did lead me here because it gave him an advantage."

"Well," Clint said, "given the kind of man he is, he can't have the entire town behind him."

"Unless," J. D. Land said, "it's that kind of town."

Clint was saddling Duke when Miranda woke up. Land handed her a cup of coffee and she walked over to Clint with it.

"Good morning," he said.

"Good morning. I want to apologize about last night."

He stopped what he was doing to look at her.

"What did you do last night that needs apologizing for?"

"Your question—I didn't answer it."

He smiled.

"You don't have to answer all my questions, Miranda," he said. "Your business is your business."

"I just . . . there are things I can't explain . . . right now."

"That's fine," he said. "I was just making conversation last night. Don't worry about it."

He went back to saddling Duke.

"Do you think this is really a good idea?" she asked.

"What? Me going into town alone?"

She nodded.

"Sure," he said, "I'll attract less attention that way."

"But if that town is full of Arnie Pace's friends—"

"I'll find that out when I get there," he said, cutting her off. He pulled the cinch tight on the saddle and dropped the stirrup into place. Then he turned and looked at her again.

"If I see that I'm significantly outnumbered," he told her, "I'll leave and come back here."

"All right."

"Just don't worry about me," he said. "Everything will work out."

Clint walked Duke over to where Land was standing.

"I'll see you both in a while," he said.

"An hour," Land said. "If you're not back in a hour we're coming in."

"Okay."

He mounted up and looked down at them.

"Better make it an hour and fifteen minutes. It'll take me a few minutes to get there."

"Done," Land said, "but no longer."

"See you both later," Clint said, and he rode toward Grand Forks.

FORTY

Arnie Pace woke early that morning. There was a girl in bed with him, but he couldn't remember who she was or how she came to be there. She was lying on her left side, naked, and he didn't see a bruise on her. He tried to control those urges while he was in Grand Forks and, consequently, sexual encounters were less than memorable for him. However, he knew from past experience that women appreciated his stamina, and he didn't expect any less from this one.

There were very fine blonde hairs where her twin cheeks met, which led him to believe she was blonde. He slapped her on the rump to wake her, then shivered when he saw the imprint of his hand on her pale skin. She squealed, and it took all of his willpower not to hit her again.

"Jesus," she said, "is that the way you wake a girl up?"

"Is there another way?" he asked. He still hadn't seen her face and still couldn't remember her.

When she rolled over he saw that she was pretty enough, with a nose that was a bit too big. Her breasts, however, were large and pale. She was not at all the type of woman he usually went to bed with, but he supposed her size hadn't mattered, since he had had no plan—he didn't *think* he'd had a plan—to bruise her.

"I can show you how I wake a man up," she offered. She reached down to stroke his penis, which reacted immediately.

"Well, then," he said, "go ahead and show me, girl."

"Norma knows how to wake a man up," she said, sliding down until she was crouched between his legs.

Norma? He thought, but then he was in her mouth, and it didn't matter what her name was.

Paxton Lewis woke up alone. He'd had his eye on a big, blond saloon girl last night, but she had left with Arnie—and she wasn't even his type!

He got out of bed, stretched and then walked to the window to look out. That was when he saw the man riding down the street. He didn't recognize him, but that didn't matter because he'd never seen Clint Adams or J. D. Land. As a matter of fact, since he didn't live in Grand Forks, he had no idea whether or not this man was a stranger. He could have been a resident, or a hand from a nearby ranch.

There was something, however, in the way the man sat his horse that told Pax that the man was neither. He hurriedly dressed to go downstairs and see if he could find out who the man was.

It was odd. Clint could usually feel when somebody was looking at him. There was absolutely no one on the street, but he still felt as if he was being watched, probably from a window.

He had little time to waste with amenities, so he decided not to go to the livery. He decided his best bet was to find the sheriff and feel the man out about how he felt about Arnie Pace. If there was no friendship there, then he'd be able to talk to the lawman more candidly about what he and the others were doing.

He spotted the sheriff's office and directed Duke over to it.

When Pax came out of the hotel, he saw the big black gelding in front of the sheriff's office. He remembered that Clint Adams rode a black gelding. It was part of all the stories that had been told about him. He didn't want to run up to Arnie with an assumption, so he decided to sit back and wait until he knew for sure.

Sheriff Frank Cantrell looked up from his desk when the door to his office opened. Clint knew the man's name because it was on a shingle outside his door. He had lots of shiny black hair, a black mustache, black beard stubble and beady eyes with heavy black eyebrows. His sleeves were rolled up to reveal hairy forearms, and there was a tuft of hair sticking out of his shirt, right at the base of his throat. He looked to be in his late forties, and Clint had the feeling this was the hairiest man he had ever seen.

"Sheriff Cantrell?"

"That's me," Cantrell said, sitting back as his chair made a loud squeak. "What can I do for you, stranger?"

"I just rode into town," Clint said. "This is my first stop."

"Well, I appreciate that, friend," Cantrell said. "Is there somethin' on your mind?"

"There is," Clint said. "My name is Clint Adams."

"Clint . . . Adams?"

"That's right."

"The Gunsmith Adams?"

"Yes."

"Well, I'll be. I ain't never been this close to a legend before. Come some closer so I kin take a good look."

Clint moved closer to the man's desk.

"You look much like any other man," the lawman said.

"That's true."

"Well, what are you doing in Grand Forks, Adams?"

"Just passing through," Clint said, "and I wanted you to know I'm not looking for any trouble."

"Well, I appreciate that, too."

"I was worried about one thing, though."

"And what's that?"

"Well," Clint said, "I was told that Arnie Pace might be up in this area. I understand he was born here."

"He was."

"Well, since he's got a reputation of his own," Clint said, "I thought it might be, uh, dangerous to stay around if he was already here."

"You afraid of ol' Arnie?"

"Not afraid," Clint said. "Like I told you, I'm not looking for any trouble."

"Why do you think Arnie would give you trouble?"

"Well, his reputation—"

"There you go again with that reputation talk," Cantrell said. "This must be somethin' he got down south. We ain't heard much about it up here. What kind of reputation would that be?"

"Well, folks say he's pretty handy with a gun."

"That's probably right."

"I wouldn't want him trying to prove a point with me while I'm here," Clint explained.

"I don't think Arnie will do that," Cantrell said. "Not in my town."

"I imagine he's got lots of friends in this town."

"Lots."

"Does that include you?"

"I'm a little older than Arnie," Cantrell said. "We didn't run together when he was young. Actually, by the time he left here I was already a deputy. No, I'm not one of Arnie's friends."

Good, Clint thought.

"Well, I just wanted to tell you that I'll try to avoid trouble while I'm here."

"Why don't you just keep going?"

"My horse needs a rest," Clint said. "I need a drink and a meal."

"You came riding in pretty early," Cantrell said. "You must have camped right outside of town."

"I didn't see any light," Clint said explained. "Believe me, when I woke up and saw your town I was surprised."

"Uh-huh. Well, thanks for checking in with me, Adams."

"Sure thing," Clint said. "I always try to check in with the local law."

He turned and walked to the door but stopped with his hand on the knob.

"By the way . . ."

"Yeah?"

"You never did tell me if Pace was in town."

Cantrell hesitated and then said, "No, I didn't."

Clint took that as a yes.

Pax watched Clint Adams leave the sheriff's office and pause just outside. Pax had seen a lot of men who made their way with a gun, and they all looked the part in the way they wore it. This man looked the part.

Clint hesitated, unsure of which way to go. The saloon was closed, so maybe the hotel was the logical next step.

Pax saw Clint step into the street, leaving his horse behind, and walk over to the hotel—to where he was sitting. It was all he could do not to get up and go inside, but that would have drawn attention to himself.

Instead, he stood his ground, trying to look comfortable as Clint Adams drew abreast of him and entered the hotel without a word.

Once Clint was inside, Pax stood up and walked across to the sheriff's office.

FORTY-ONE

Clint noticed the man sitting in a chair in front of the hotel. He knew the man was watching him. When he went by the man to enter the hotel, he pointedly ignored him. Once he was inside, he walked to the front window to see what the man would do. He watched him as he crossed the street and entered the sheriff's office.

He turned and looked at the man behind the desk. He was one of the biggest men he'd ever seen. Judging from what the sheriff had said, this man looked about Arnie Pace's age.

"Can I help you?" the man asked. "Looking for a room?"

Clint decided to be truthful and see what happened.

"I'm looking for Arnie Pace."

"Oh?"

"Do you know him?"

"Sure, I know him," the man said. "He was born here."

"Is he registered in the hotel?"

"Nope."

"Is he in town?"

"I couldn't say."

"Is he a friend of yours?"

"Yes," the man said. "Is he a friend of yours?"

Clint hesitated a moment and then said, "More like a friend of a friend."

"Why are you looking for him?"

"To say hello."

The man nodded, not taking his eyes off Clint.

"Well, tell me your name, and if I see Arnie, I'll give him the message."

"My name is Clint Adams," Clint said. "If you see him, just tell him I'm looking for him."

"And the reason you're looking for him is . . . ?"

"He'll know."

"I'll tell him," the man said, "but let me give you some advice, friend, since you're a stranger here."

"I always like to hear advice."

"Arnie's got a lot of friends in this town," the clerk said. "We don't care what he's done anywhere else in the country, he's never done anything here but be a good friend."

"Is that a fact?"

"It is," the man said, "it is a fact."

"The whole town feels that way?"

The man hesitated, then said, "Pretty much."

Now Clint knew the man was lying. He wanted Clint to think he'd be taking on a whole town if he tried anything.

"Well," Clint said, "thanks for the advice. I'll keep it in mind."

He turned to leave.

"Hey."

"Yeah?" he asked.

"Where should I tell Arnie you'll be?" he asked. "You know, if he wants to see you."

Clint thought a moment and then said, "Just tell him that I'll be around."

"I'll do that."

"Thanks."

• • •

"Why are you askin' me questions?" Sheriff Frank Cantrell asked Paxton Lewis.

"I told you, Sheriff," Pax said. "Arnie Pace wants to know."

"Well, if Arnie wants to know anything from me," Cantrell said, "you tell him to come and ask me himself."

"I was just asking about the stranger in town," Pax said. "What's the big deal?"

"Mister," Cantrell said, "there's more than one stranger in town."

"But I'm Arnie's friend."

"That don't make you any less a stranger to me."

"Arnie's not gonna like this."

"If he don't," Cantrell said, "tell him to take it up with me."

"But—"

"Time for you to leave, friend."

Pax stood his ground for a moment and then turned and walked to the door.

Clint left the hotel convinced that Arnie Pace was, indeed, in town. He didn't wait to see the other man come out of the sheriff's office. He was satisfied that Pace was somewhere in town, that he had friends in town, but that the entire town, and probably the local law, would not back his play.

He mounted Duke and rode back out of town. He would arrive back in camp with ten minutes to spare.

When Pax came out of the sheriff's office the big gelding was gone. He looked up and down the street but didn't see him. Before reporting to Arnie, though, he was going to have to talk to Bear, to see what Clint Adams had done in the hotel.

If it was even Clint Adams.

FORTY-TWO

When the knock came at his door, Arnie Pace left the bed and the warm, willing girl who was in it.

"Arnie," Bear Morgan said, "sorry to bother you."

"What is it, Bear?"

"There was a fella here lookin' for you just now."

"Who was it?"

"Said his name was Clint Adams."

"Adams," Pace said, nodding.

"You know who he is?"

"Sure, I know."

"I read about him," Bear said. "What's a famous gunman want with you?"

"Well," Pace said, "I guess the best way to find that out is to ask him, don't ya think?"

"Sure, Arnie."

"Where is he, Bear?"

"He just said to tell you he'll be around."

"Well, then, I guess I'll get to talk to him sooner or later. Did you tell him I was here?"

"No," Bear said. "I told him I'd pass on his message if I saw you."

"That's good, Bear," Pace said, "that was really good. Can you do another favor for me?"

"Sure, Arnie. Just tell me what you want."

"Find Pax for me and send him up."

"I saw him a little while ago," Bear said. "I'll get him for you."

"Okay . . . and Bear?"

"Yeah?"

"Thanks for the information."

Bear nodded and withdrew.

Arnie Pace closed the door, turned to the girl on the bed and said, "Get dressed. Time for you to go."

When Pax reentered the hotel, Bear told him Arnie wanted to see him. On the way up the stairs he passed the big blonde coming down. There wasn't a mark on her.

When he reached Pace's door he knocked.

"Come in, Pax."

Pax opened the door, entered and closed the door behind him. Arnie Pace was standing at the window with his back to Pax.

"Why did I have to find out from Bear that Clint Adams was in town?" he demanded.

Instantly, Pax was angry with Bear for jumping the gun.

"I was tryin' to find out if it was him," Pax said.

"How were you doin' that?"

"I talked to the sheriff, because that's where . . . where the stranger went when he came into town."

"And?"

"The sheriff wouldn't help," Pax said. "He wouldn't confirm or deny that it was Adams."

"Well, Bear found out it was him. Do you know how?"

"How?"

"From Adams himself," Pax said.

He turned and stared at Pax.

"Why didn't you go right up to Adams and ask him?"

"That would have given us away, Arnie," Pax said. "I didn't want to give us away."

"If he's here it's because he tracked us," Pace said.

"But why?" Pax asked. "What's he got against us?"

"I don't know," Pace said, "but I'm not gonna let him ruin this for me. I want J. D. Land with no complications. So do you know what we're gonna do?"

"What?"

"We're gonna get rid of that complication," Pace said.

"You mean . . . kill the Gunsmith?"

"That's right."

"Just us?"

"There are plenty of men in this town who will help," Pace said, "but I'm gonna have to talk to them myself."

"And what do you want me to do, Arnie?"

"You're gonna have to find out where Adams is, Pax," Pace said, "because we can't kill him if we don't know that, right?"

"Right."

"Don't push him," Pace said, "just find him, tell him I want to see him, too, and that I'll be in touch. You got that?"

"I got it, Arnie."

"Good," Pace said. "Then go ahead and get it done. When you get back, I'll let you know how many men we have backing us up."

Pax nodded and left. Pace turned again to look out the window. If he hadn't been busy with the woman he might have seen Adams ride in himself. As much as he liked Grand Forks and thought of it as home, being here took away his edge.

That was going to have to change.

FORTY-THREE

By the time Clint reached the camp, even with those ten minutes to spare, Land and Miranda had saddled their horses.

"He's back!" Miranda called as Clint rode up to them. Then she directed herself to him. "Is he there? Is Arnie Pace there?"

Clint dismounted and said, "I believe he is."

"You believe?" she asked.

"You didn't see him?" Land asked.

"No," Clint said, "but no one would say whether he was or wasn't." He told them of his talk with the sheriff and the desk clerk, and then about the man who'd been sitting in front of the hotel when he got there.

"He must be there," Clint said, "and now he knows I'm looking for him."

"What will he do?" Miranda asked.

"He'll probably try to get rid of me before J. D. gets here."

"And what do we do?" she asked.

"We go in and get him," Land said, "no matter how many others we have to go through."

Clint told them what he thought, that they would not be facing an entire town, or the law, in his opinion.

"How do we do this?" Miranda asked.

"I'll go in first, again, but you two follow soon after. They won't expect a man and a woman together."

"What if they attack you as soon as you ride in?" Miranda asked.

"I've been pretty good a dodging bullets all these years," he told her, "but I think he'll probably want to talk first."

"Talk?" she asked. "About what?"

"Well, if you knew a man was after you, a man you didn't know and had never met," Clint asked, "wouldn't you want to know why?"

"Why won't he just think it's for the reward?" she asked.

"Because," he said, "I have a reputation as a lot of things, but a bounty hunter is not one of them."

He looked at Land.

"All right," the other man said. "Go ahead. We'll be ten minutes behind you. No more."

"That's good," Clint said. He looked at Miranda. "You may have to show us how good you are with that rifle."

"I'm ready," she said.

"Okay, then," Clint said. "Good luck to us all. Let's hope we all walk away from this."

He remounted Duke and rode back to town.

Pax couldn't locate Clint or the big gelding, and just as he was about to give up, they came riding back into town. He took a deep breath, kept his hand away from his gun and stepped into the street.

Clint saw the man, recognized him from the hotel, and surmised from his demeanor that this was not a challenge.

He and Duke stopped right in front of the man.

"Clint Adams?"

"That's right. And who are you?"

"Paxton Lewis."

"Ah ha," Clint said. "Arnie Pace's man."

"Partner."

"Right. What can I do for you, Arnie's partner?"

"Arnie would like to have a word with you."

"Is that a fact? When?"

"Today."

"Where?"

That stumped Pax.

"I got to tell him you're willin'," he said, "and then he'll have me tell you where."

"Okay, then," Clint said. "Go and tell him I'm willing."

"Where will you be?"

"Right here."

"In the middle of the street?"

"I figure if you had a man on the roof with a rifle I'd know it by now," Clint said, "so I'll just wait right here."

"Okay," Pax said, "suit yourself," and he crossed the street to the hotel.

Arnie Pace looked out his window and saw the Gunsmith sitting on his horse in the street.

"Sonofabitch, he *is* there," he said. "I haven't even had time to round up some help."

He turned and looked at Pax.

"You're gonna have to do it for me."

"I don't know the people in this town."

"I'll tell you who to go to," Pace said. "Just tell Adams to meet me in the saloon."

"When?"

"In one hour."

"Will it be open?"

"I'll make sure it's open."

"You gonna meet him alone?"

"Alone," Pace said, "man to man."

"Good luck, Arnie," Pax said, and left.

Pace turned to look out the window again.

FORTY-FOUR

Paxton Lewis stepped onto the street to deliver the message to Clint, who had already caught someone looking out the hotel window at him.

"In the saloon," he said to Clint, "in one hour."

"Will it be open?"

"Don't worry," Pax said, "it'll be open."

"Will you be there?"

Pax shook his head.

"I have other things I have to take care of."

"So it'll just be me and Pace?"

"Just you and Arnie," Pax said.

"I'll be there."

Pax nodded but then felt awkward. What should he do? Go back to the hotel or just walk away? In the end, he chose to walk away and run the errands given him by Pace.

Clint turned Duke around and walked him back to the saloon. He didn't know what talking with Arnie Pace would accomplish, other than giving Land and Miranda time to get into town. He didn't think anything could be said that would head off the inevitable bloodbath.

It was too early for the saloon to be open, but Clint assumed that one of Pace's "friends" probably ran it.

He dismounted, sat in a chair in front of the place and waited for the door to open.

The town started to come awake as Clint sat there. Businesses opened, people came out onto the street, and in the middle of it all, J. D. Land and Miranda rode into town. As expected, they did not draw an inordinate amount of attention. A few people glanced at the strangers, but no one stared.

Land and Miranda rode right by Clint, apparently without giving him a look. He knew, however, that they were looking, so he simply jerked his thumb at the saloon, hoping they'd catch his meaning. Eventually, they rode out of sight, but he knew he'd see them soon.

"Did you catch that?" Land asked as he and Miranda rode to the other end of town.

"Catch what?"

"Clint was indicating that he's going to meet Arnie in the saloon."

"He did that?" she asked. "I didn't notice."

"I did."

"What do we do?"

Land reined his horse in and looked at her.

"We leave our horses here and go back on foot."

"Shouldn't we give him time to talk to Arnie?" she asked.

"What for?" Land asked. "Is Arnie going to say something that's going to keep him alive?"

"No," she said, "nothing will keep him safe from me."

"Or from me," Land said.

They dismounted, and Land checked the loads in his gun. Miranda did the same with her rifle.

"You're not going to be afraid to use that, are you?" he asked.

"Just wait and see."

"I'd rather know now."

She gave him a hard look.

"I'll be there when you need me."

He stared back at her and then said, "Good enough."

Arnie Pace had everything set for the saloon. As he had expected, his friends were very willing to help him. Those who weren't—well, they weren't his friends, anymore, and they'd stay out of the way.

He'd gotten the key to the saloon and used it on the back door. When everything was in place, he went to the front doors and opened them. Clint stood up and looked expectantly at the doorway.

"Clint Adams?" Pace asked.

"That's right."

"Arnie Pace."

"I figured as much."

"Come on in so we can talk."

Arnie backed away from the doorway and Clint went through the batwing doors. By this time Arnie was behind the bar.

"Drink?" Pace was holding a bottle of whiskey.

"It's a little early for me," Clint said, "but I'll have a beer."

Something was wrong. He could feel it.

Pace drew him a beer and set it on the bar. He then poured himself a whiskey.

"To first meetings," he said, holding his glass out.

Clint walked to the bar, picked up the beer with his left hand and said, "To first meetings."

They clinked glasses, Pace also using his left hand.

"Very good," he said. "Always keep your gunhand empty."

Clint didn't respond.

"All right," Pace said, "you wanted to see me. Why?"

"J. D. Land's family."

"What about them?"

"You killed them."

"So?"

"Raped his wife."

"Again, so?"

"Shot his little—"

"I *know* what I did, Adams," Pace said. "Why are you here?"

"I'm trying to keep J. D. from killing you."

"You mean Reverend Land?" A mean smile spread over his face.

"Not the Reverend," Clint said. "That man died when you slaughtered his family. The man who is after you is J. D. Land."

"That man died ten years ago," Pace said. "Do you know what that means?"

"What?"

"I'm being hunted by a man with no name."

"No," Clint said, "if we're both right, then you're being hunted by a dead man."

Pace frowned, sipped his whiskey, and then said, "Well, that is somethin' to think about, ain't it?"

FORTY-FIVE

Land and Miranda decided to take it slowly walking back to the saloon, which turned out to be a good idea.

"Uh-oh," Land said, putting out a hand to stop her.

She didn't have to ask what he meant because she, too, saw the men in front of the saloon.

"I guess Arnie didn't want to meet him alone," she said.

"I wouldn't have expected him to," Land said. "Three in the front. I wonder how many in the back?"

"Or inside?"

They looked at each other.

"We've got to help him," Miranda finally said.

"And we will. You stay here."

"Where are you going?"

"Around the back to see how many men there are."

She grabbed hold of his sleeve and pulled hard.

"Don't even think about goin' in there without me, J. D.," she hissed, angrily. "I mean it."

"I know you do, Miranda," he said. "Now let go of my shirt."

After a long moment she let him go.

• • •

Pax was on the outside of the saloon with two men who had been supplied by Bear Morgan. He knew that there were also three in the back. He didn't know how many Arnie had taken inside with him.

He had the feeling that these men were doing this more for Bear than for Arnie Pace. Arnie couldn't have that many friends . . . could he?

"When do we go?" one of the men asked.

"At the sound of the first shot," Pax said, "not before."

"And we only have to handle one man?"

"That's right."

"Who is he?"

Pax looked at the man.

"Nobody told you?"

"No," the man said, "just that we'd be handling a stranger."

Pax hesitated, but it was too late to get away with *not* telling them who they were up against.

"It's Clint Adams."

The man froze, then looked at Pax.

"We ain't gettin' paid enough," the man finally said.

"Who's payin' you?"

"Bear."

"Then take it up with him."

"I will."

"After we're done here."

"If we're still alive," the man mumbled.

Definitely not one of Arnie's friends.

Land worked his way around to the back of saloon and saw what he'd expected. Clint was effectively sealed inside. There were three men gathered around the back door, and all were armed. If he tried to take them now it would alert everyone, and there'd be a bloodbath. Also, what if he wasn't the J. D. Land he was ten years ago? To try to take these three men would be risking his life *without* ever having his shot at Arnie Pace.

He withdrew to give Miranda the news.

"So what do we do?" she asked.

"I've got a plan."

"What is it?"

"Well," he said, slowly, "it involves . . ."

"Involves what?" she asked. She swore he looked embarrassed. "Come on, J. D., spit it out."

"Well," he said, "it involves you being . . . um, a little . . . uh . . . naked."

She put her hands on her hips and said, "Is that all?"

"How about some poker?" Pace asked.

"Two-handed?"

"Sure," Pace said. "Poker calms me down, and I understand you play."

"A little."

Pace came out from under the bar with a deck of cards.

"Right here at the bar," he said.

"Fine."

"Only let's play for high stakes."

"How high did you have in mind?"

Pace riffled the deck and asked, "How about life and death."

Clint grinned and said, "Sort of gives the phrase 'high stakes' a whole new meaning."

Pace also grinned and said, "I knew you'd understand."

FORTY-SIX

"Are you sure you're all right with this?" Land asked Miranda.

"I'm fine."

"I mean, I could try to think of something else."

"No!" she said, quickly. "You came up with this one. I'd hate to see what you'll come up with to replace it."

"Well . . ."

"Are you sure you were a reverend?"

"Only for ten years."

"Oh, well," she said, unbuttoning her shirt, "that's different, then."

She removed her shirt as if it was not there, handed it to him as if he were a nail on a wall and then went to work on her undergarments. Before long she was standing before him, naked to the waist, breasts quite full and beautiful. Land didn't know where to look. In ten years he had never seen a naked woman except for his Miriam, who had smaller but no less lovely breasts. Also, Miriam's skin was whiter than Miranda's.

"What is it?" Miranda asked.

"Hmm? What?"

"You look like you're about to cry."

"No," he said, huskily, "not really. I was just . . . thinking."

"About your wife?"

"Yes."

"Do I look like her?"

"No."

There was a slight breeze playing across Miranda's bare flesh, and it made her nipples pucker. What she was about to do excited her, and her breathing was coming faster. She was surprised to find that she was aroused—and the only man available at the moment was an ex-preacher!

"You're . . . lovely," he said. "She was . . . lovely."

"Why don't we forget about the past for now," she suggested, "and get this over with."

"Good idea," he said. "We don't want something to happen before we're ready."

"Right."

She picked up her shirt and put it back on, but did not tuck the tails in. It would soon be coming off again, anyway.

Inside the saloon, Clint and Arnie Pace were still discussing the ground rules of their game. Clint still wasn't sure what to do now that he was face-to-face with the man he, Land and Miranda had been chasing. How was he going to keep one of those two from killing him—and why should he?

But there was still something wrong in the saloon. He could feel it, almost smell it, and then he knew what it was.

They weren't alone.

"I'm surprised you don't have some of your friends in here with guns," Clint said.

"Why would I?" Pace asked. "Am I in danger from you?"

"In danger, yes," Clint said. "But not from me—unless you make that choice."

"You're talkin' about Land?" Pace asked. "I could have taken him ten years ago, and I can take him now."

"You think so?"

"I know so," Pace said. "You don't just pick up a gun after ten years and take up where you left off."

"Maybe," Clint said, "if you're a special kind of man, you do."

"Ah!" Pace said. "There ain't nothin' special about J. D. Land. He's just a man, like me, like you—well, maybe not like you."

"What do you mean?"

"Well, you *are* special."

Clint couldn't believe his ears. Was he being complimented by Arnie Pace?

"You know what I mean," Pace said. "You got yourself a big rep. You're a legend!"

"I'm no legend."

"No? Everybody else seems to think so."

"If that's true, then I admire you," Clint said.

"You admire me?" Pace asked. "Why?"

"You had the courage to come here and meet me alone," Clint said. "Another man, a lesser man than you, would have been to afraid to do that. He would have brought help. Probably would have put some men in front of the saloon, some men at the back door, and even brought some of them right in here, hiding someplace. But not you. You've got guts."

Pace was staring at Clint while he spoke, glaring actually, because he knew what Clint was doing. He was making fun of him, because he sensed that there were others in the saloon.

"Guts," Pace said. "The graveyard's full of men who had guts. It's brains that count, Adams, and that's what I have. Brains."

"Meaning?"

"Meaning I wasn't stupid enough to come here alone, just as you suspect. But I'm still gonna give you a chance."

"What chance is that, Arnie?"

Pace slapped the deck of cards down on the bar.

"One hand of showdown," he said, "winner take all."

"What's all?"

Pace grinned. "Now that's somethin' we got to talk about."

FORTY-SEVEN

Land hid in an alley, from where he could see the back of the saloon. Miranda starting walking toward the three men who were set up at the back door. Her hips were swaying and she exuded an air of sexuality that even J. D. Land felt. As he watched her walk his mouth felt dry.

"Hello, boys."

The three men turned and looked at her, and their expressions became like those of a child on Christmas morning.

"Well, hello, darlin'," one of them said.

Land couldn't see, but her breasts were swaying loosely beneath her shirt, and she even had a couple of buttons undone so the men could see the slopes of her breasts.

"What are you fellas doin' out here?" she asked.

"Waitin' for you, darlin'," the same man said. He seemed to be spokesman. They were all in their mid-thirties or so and were extremely susceptible to Miranda's charms.

"Well," she said, touching the spokesman's arm, "a girl sure likes to have big, strong, handsome men waiting for her."

"What's your name, sweet thing?" the man asked.

"Oh, names," she said, wrinkling her nose. She turned and stroked one of the other men under his chin. "Names just get in the way, don't they?"

"They sure do," the second man said.

"I think," Miranda said, "we should just be men and women, here, and do what men and women do."

The three men exchanged glances, and their faces told the tale. They couldn't believe their luck.

"Are you sayin'—" the third man started.

"You know what I'm sayin', handsome."

"You mean," the first man said, "all three of us?"

"Sure," she said, smiling, maneuvering around them in order to put their backs to Land. "Why not? The more the merrier."

It was at that moment she undid the remaining buttons on her shirt and let it slide down her shoulders. Three jaws dropped at the sight of her full breasts with their puckered nipples.

"Who's gonna be first?" she asked.

"Me!" the first man said.

"No, me," the second said.

"Why you?" asked the third one.

"Boys, boys," she said, "before any one of you can come over here, you got to get rid of those guns."

"Our guns?" the second man asked.

"You don't have to *get rid* of them," she said, "just sort of . . . drop them to the ground."

"But—but where are we going to . . ." the first man asked.

"Right here, big boy," Miranda said, running her hands over her breasts, "right here against this wall, while your friends watch—and then it'll be their turn."

"Les," the second man said to the first, "we're supposed to be helpin' Arnie—"

"Arnie can take care of himself," the man named Les said. He undid his gunbelt and let it drop to the floor.

Land held his breath as the other two men did the same thing, and then they started moving in on Miranda.

"Hey," she said, "I figured one at a time."

"You figured wrong," Les said. "See, none of us wants to watch."

By this time Land was behind them with his gun drawn.

"I'm afraid the fun's over, boys," he said.

The three men froze, then looked behind them.

"What is this?" Les asked.

Miranda put her shirt back on and pushed past the three men. She picked up their gunbelts and went to stand by Land.

"What's goin' on?" the second man asked. "I thought we wuz gonna—is this your husband?"

"Not my husband," Miranda said, "just a friend of mine helping me keep lice like you off me."

"Who you callin' names, you bi—" Les started, but Land cut him off by cocking the hammer back on his gun.

"We can do this the easy way," Land said, "or the hard way."

"What's the easy way?" Les asked.

"That's the way you stay alive."

The three men looked at each other, and then Les shrugged and said, "I'm all for stayin' alive. I ain't ready to die for no Arnie Pace."

"Hell," one of the other men said, "I don't even like him."

"Okay, Mister," Les said, "we'll take the easy way."

"Don't you even want to know what the hard way is?" Land asked.

"Naw," Les said, "I think we pretty much got it figured out what the hard way is, don't we, boys?"

The other men nodded in agreement.

"Good," Land said, "then it's time for you boys to turn around."

"Turn around?" Les asked.

"That's right."

"You ain't gonna kill us?"

"No," Land said, "We just need you out of the way for a while."

"How far out of the wa—" Les started, but he was the first man Land hit with his gun. The other two soon followed Les to the ground.

"Toss those guns away," Land told Miranda.

"I'll toss two of them," she said, throwing them over a fence, "but I think I'll use the other one."

She strapped on the holster, which did not look very natural attached to her leg.

"You, uh, can button up now," Land said.

"Oh," she said, looking down at herself, "yeah."

Damn if she wasn't still aroused. What was wrong with her? There was work to be done.

"What do we do now?" she asked, buttoning the shirt all the way to the top button. Land was pleased. He didn't have her breasts as a distraction anymore.

"My guess is that this back door is unlocked to allow these men to go inside if they have to," Land said. "That's what we're going to do."

"What about the men in front?" she asked.

"Hopefully," he said, "it'll all be over before they can get into the action."

"What about Arnie?" she asked.

"What about him?"

"Who gets to kill him, you or me?"

"Why don't we wait until we get inside and see what's what and then decide?" he suggested. "Clint's already been in there alone for too long."

"Okay," she said, looking down at the unconscious men. "Let's do it before these fellas wake up."

FORTY-EIGHT

Out in front, the two men with Pax were getting impatient and nervous now that they knew who they had to face.

"What the hell are they doin' in there?" one asked.

"Arnie knows what he's doin'," Pax said. "Just relax."

"You tell us we're goin' up against the Gunsmith, and you want us to relax?" the second man asked. He'd been informed by the first man.

"He's just another man," Pax said. "Besides, Arnie will probably take care of him himself. We may not even have to go in."

"I'm for that," the first man said. "Bear Morgan's gonna owe me plenty for this little job."

"Just be ready to go if we have to," Pax said.,

"Yeah," the first man said, and exchanged a glance with the second man.

Land and Miranda moved down a hall that led from the back door to the saloon's main room. It was a curtained doorway, rather than one with a door, so they were able to peek out.

"Jesus," Miranda said. "There's four guys crouched down behind the bar."

"I see them."

"But does Clint know they're there?"

"He probably feels something isn't right," Land said. "They're not going to surprise him."

"No," she said, "just outnumber him."

Land looked at her and said, "That's what we're here for."

"Look at Arnie," she said, in disgust. Puffed up like a peacock."

"I am looking at him," Land said, and he was surprised at not only the depth of his hatred for the man, but his revulsion as well.

Miranda was feeling just about the same thing.

"I could hit him from here," she said.

"You might hit Clint."

"Well, what are they doing?"

"It looks like . . . uh, yes, it looks like they're . . . playing poker."

"Poker?"

"Let's listen," he said.

"If I win," Arnie Pace said, "you have to ride with me."

"And what if I win?"

"Then you get to kill me," Pace said, and then added, "if you can."

"You know what, Arnie?"

"What?"

"I think you're a loser," Clint said. "I think you've been a loser all your life, and I think you're going to lose now."

"Oh, yeah?" Pace sneered. "Does that mean you're takin' my bet?"

"I'm taking it, all right. Deal the cards."

Pace shuffled the deck once when Clint said, "Not that deck."

Pace stopped.

"Why not?"

"I want to crack a fresh deck."

"We ain't got a fresh deck."

"There's got to be one here somewhere," Clint said. "Want me to come around and help you look?"

"Are you sayin' you think I cheat at cards?"

"Arnie," Clint said, "you steal and rape and kill, so what's a little cheating?"

For a moment, Clint thought Pace was going to take offense, but in the end the man smiled and said, "You got a point there. Okay, a fresh deck. Lemme see. Ah, here's one."

He brought out a deck of cards and let Clint look at it. The seal was still intact, and Clint approved the new deck.

Pace cracked it, brought the cards out and began to shuffle them.

"I'll let you choose the game," he said to Clint.

"Five-card stud," Clint said. "It'll be quicker that way."

"Maybe," Pace said, "but I want to take it slow. Here's the first two cards."

He dealt the face-down card, then the first face-up card. He had a king, Clint a three.

"Uh-oh," he said, chuckling, "give it up now, Adams."

"Just deal."

"Third card," Pace said, and dealt it out. He got another king, Clint another three.

"Hmm," Pace said, "interesting, don't you think?"

"You talk too much."

"If we were playin' for real money would you call a bet at this point?" Pace asked.

"I'm playin' for life or death," Clint said. "What do you think I'd do? Come on, deal."

"Fourth card," Pace said.

"Why are they playin' poker?" Miranda demanded.

"Well, from what I can hear," Land said, "they're playin' for life or death."

"What?" Miranda asked. "I hope Arnie doesn't think he's gonna get away if he wins a hand of poker."

"Clint's tryin' to force his hand by humiliating him."

"But how does Clint know he's gonna win?"

"Because Arnie's a loser and always has been."

They both gave their attention back to the poker game.

Pace's fourth card was a jack. Clint's was a seven.

"One card left," Arnie Pace said. "Still in the game, Adams?"

"I'm always in the game, Arnie," Clint said. "Let's see the last card."

Pace shrugged and pitched it out there. He got another jack for two pair. Clint got a useless deuce.

"Two pair," Pace said, putting the deck down. "Pretty hard to beat."

"Yep," Clint said, "pretty hard to beat, except that you're a loser, Arnie. You turn even a winning hand into a losing one. What I wish I could do is raise the hand."

"You'd raise against this hand?" Pace asked, pointing to his cards on the table.

"What if I got a king or a jack underneath. You can't possibly beat a full house. If we were playin' for real money, you'd fold."

"Not a chance, Arnie," Clint said.

"Why not?"

"Because you don't have a jack or a king."

"If we were playing for real," Pace growled, "I'd make you pay for the privilege."

He turned over his hole card, and it was just a useless six.

"Two pair," he said. "Beat it."

"Before I turn my card over, Arnie, I want you to know something."

"What's that?"

"If those friends of yours who are here, hidden someplace—maybe even behind the bar with you—jump up with their guns blazing, my first bullet's going to find you."

"Why the threats, Adams?" Pace asked. "We're just playin' a friendly game of poker—you know, like two friends."

"You're not any friend of mine, Arnie," Clint said. "Besides, I really don't associate . . . with losers."

Clint turned over his hole card, which was a third three.

The winning hand.

"You lose," Clint said.

"Boys!" Pace shouted, and fell to the floor behind the bar.

FORTY-NINE

Behind the curtained doorway Land said, "Let's move."

Clint backed away from the bar as four men sprang up from their crouched positions. However, Pace had taken so much time with Clint that the men were all suffering from aching knees. They stood, but they couldn't move very well. They looked like ducks in a shooting gallery.

Clint had no way of knowing which of them were good with a gun, so he simply started on the left. He shot the first man in the chest, and then the second got a bullet through his forehead.

By that time, Land and Miranda were in the room, firing their guns. The third and fourth men succumbed to a barrage of bullets.

When it was over, there was a brief moment of silence, except for the sound of Miranda's gun hammer falling on empty chambers.

"That's enough, Miranda," Land said.

Miranda stopped pulling the trigger on the empty gun and dropped it to the floor. She'd had her rifle in her other hand the whole time, so now she grasped it firmly in both, because it wasn't over yet.

"Clint!" Land said. "The front!"

Clint turned just as three men came charging into the saloon, screaming like banshees. They fired, and Clint, Land, and Miranda fired. Pax was first through the door, and Clint put one in his gut. He heard Land's handgun go off and then Miranda's rifle, and the other two men fell dead.

"Any more?" Clint asked.

"Three out back," Land said, "but we took them out of play."

"So," Clint said, "that leaves Arnie."

Before any of them could say another word, a gun and holster came flying over the bar, landing with a thud on the floor.

"That's my gun," Arnie Pace called out. "I'm gonna stand up."

"Go ahead," Clint said, holstering his own weapon.

Arnie Pace stood up with his hands in the air. He was surprisingly chipper for a man who was staring death in the face.

"Well, well, J. D. Look at you."

Land said nothing.

"And is that little Miranda? How's your sister, sweetie? Last time I saw her she wasn't lookin' too good."

"She's dead, you sonofabitch!" Miranda said. "You killed her."

"And my family," Land said. "For that you have to pay, Arnie."

"Well," Pace said, "unfortunately I'm unarmed, and if you shoot an unarmed man you could find yourself in a lot of trouble. Right Adams?"

"Normally."

"Whataya mean, normally?"

"Well, if there was a witness I guess there'd be trouble."

"What are you talkin' about?" Pace asked. "*You're* the witness."

"Me?" Clint asked. "Hell, Arnie. I'm not even here.

Never was.'' He looked at Land. ''You say there's three men in the back?''

''That's right.''

''I'd better see to them before they wake up.''

He walked toward Land and Miranda, then stopped beside them.

''Come outside with me, Miranda.''

''No.''

''J. D. will do what has to be done,'' Clint said. ''There's no need for you—''

''There is!'' she insisted. ''There is a need . . . but I thank you for offering me a way out, Clint. You're a good man.''

Clint looked at Land, who had not taken his eyes off of Arnie Pace.

''See you, Arnie,'' Clint said, and went through the curtain.

''Hey, wait a minute!'' Pace shouted. ''You can't leave me with them. They're both crazy. Hey . . . hey . . . I'm unar—''

His voice was cut off by the sound of a pistol and a rifle firing together. Clint didn't hear the body fall. He was already out back.

EPILOGUE

Clint woke the next day with Miranda's naked form next to him. They'd had some explaining to do to the sheriff, and it had taken the rest of the day. In the end, Land and Miranda supported each other's stories that Arnie Pace had gone for a gun. Clint was able to support the rest of the story, since he'd killed some of the men himself. The three men Land had knocked out were in custody.

When it got to be late, both Clint and Land turned in. They each wanted to get an early start in the morning.

Clint had not yet fallen asleep when there was a knock at his door. When he opened it, Miranda was standing in the hall, breathing heavily.

"It's either you or the Reverend," she said. "Personally, I prefer you, but if you turn me away, I'll go to his room."

"Well," Clint said, "just to keep him from having to make a painful decision . . ."

He'd grabbed her, pulled her in and kissed her. Her shirt fell open and her heavy breasts were against his chest.

"Jesus," she said, against his lips, "Jesus . . . I want it so bad. Is that what happens when you kill someone?"

"No," Clint said, kissing her sweet neck, "this is what happens when you're still alive . . . ."

They made love again in the morning, as he slid his hand down her back to the curve of her butt and then ran his middle finger along the crease between her cheeks. In his old age, Clint was becoming something of a butt expert, and she had a fine one.

He paid a lot of attention to it.

Later, while they dressed, she asked, "What's J. D. gonna do?"

"He doesn't know," Clint said. "I suspect he'll travel a bit. He feels he can't go back to Peculiar." Clint looked out the window, and at that moment J. D. Land rode past the hotel. He didn't look up or around, but kept his eyes straight ahead.

"I don't blame him."

"What about you?" he asked, turning away from the window. "What will you do?"

"I have some family back East," she said. "I guess I'll go visit them."

They finished dressing and were ready to leave. As they stepped into the hall, he asked, "All you all right with what you did, Miranda?"

"I think so," she said, thoughtfully. "I mean, I don't regret killing Arnie . . . ."

"But?"

"But it didn't taste as sweet as I thought it would."

Clint closed the hotel room door behind them and said, "Revenge never does."

Watch for

AMBUSH AT BLACK ROCK

217th novel in the exciting GUNSMITH series
from Jove

Coming in January!

30 THINGS I NEED TO TELL MY SON

FAMILY CHRISTIAN STORES
Grand Rapids, MI 49530

The quoted ideas expressed in this book (but not scripture verses) are not, in all cases, exact quotations, as some have been edited for clarity and brevity. In all cases, the author has attempted to maintain the speaker's original intent. In some cases, quoted material for this book was obtained from secondary sources, primarily print media. While every effort was made to ensure the accuracy of these sources, the accuracy cannot be guaranteed. For additions, deletions, corrections or clarifications in future editions of this text, please write FAMILY CHRISTIAN STORES.

Cover Design by Kim Russell / Wahoo Designs
Page Layout by Bart Dawson

ISBN 978-1-60587-035-9

Printed in the United States of America

. . . A MESSAGE FOR PARENTS

30 THINGS I NEED TO TELL MY SON

TABLE OF CONTENTS

INTRODUCTION
A Message to Parents

Because you're older and wiser than your son, you have much to teach him (even if he doesn't think so). But what lessons should you teach first? After all, you probably have hundreds of ideas rattling around in your brain, all of them important. And with so many things to consider, you may have found it tough to organize your thoughts. So, perhaps you haven't yet taken the time to sit down with your son and share your own personalized set of life-lessons in a systematic way. If that's the case, this book can help.

This text focuses on 30 timeless insights for Christians, lessons that your son desperately needs to hear from you. So here's your assignment: read this book, add your own personal insights in the back, and then schedule a series of face-to-face, no-interruptions-allowed, parent-to-son talks with the young guy whom God has entrusted to your care. Carve out enough time to really explore these concepts, and don't be afraid to share your own personal experiences: your victories, your defeats, and the lessons you learned along the way.

We live in a world where far too many parents have out-sourced the job of raising their kids, with predictably sour results. And make no mistake, your youngster is going to learn about life from somebody; in fact, he's learning about life every single day—some of the lessons are positive, and quite a few aren't. So ask yourself: Is your boy being tutored by the world or by you? The world will, at times, intentionally mislead your youngster, but you never will. So grab this book, grab your notes, grab your boy, and have the kind of parent-to-son talks that both of you deserve.

1

Talk to Your Son About

God's Plan

Dear Son, God Has a Plan for Your Life That's Bigger (and Better) Than Yours.

"For I know the plans I have for you"—[this is] the Lord's declaration—"plans for [your] welfare, not for disaster, to give you a future and a hope."

Jeremiah 29:11 HCSB

The Bible makes it clear: God has plans—very big plans—for you and your family. But He won't force His plans upon you—if you wish to experience the abundance that God has in store, you must be willing to accept His will and follow His Son.

As Christians, you and your family members should ask yourselves this question: "How closely can we make our plans match God's plans?" The more closely you manage to follow the path that God intends for your lives, the better.

Your son undoubtedly has concerns about his present circumstances, and you should encourage him to take those concerns to God in prayer. Your son has hopes and dreams. You should encourage him to talk to God about those dreams. And your son is making plans for the future, a future by the way, that only the Creator can see. You should ask your youngster to let God guide his steps.

So remember that God intends to use you—and your son—in wonderful, unexpected ways. And it's up to you to seek His plan for your own life while encouraging your son to do the same. When you do, you'll discover that God's plans are grand and glorious . . . more glorious than either of you can imagine.

We know that all things work together for the good of those who love God: those who are called according to His purpose.

Romans 8:28 HCSB

But as it is written: What no eye has seen and no ear has heard, and what has never come into a man's heart, is what God has prepared for those who love Him.

1 Corinthians 2:9 HCSB

In Him we were also made His inheritance, predestined according to the purpose of the One who works out everything in agreement with the decision of His will.

Ephesians 1:11 HCSB

Yet Lord, You are our Father; we are the clay, and You are our potter; we all are the work of Your hands.

Isaiah 64:8 HCSB

He replied, "Every plant that My heavenly Father didn't plant will be uprooted."

Matthew 15:13 HCSB

MORE FROM GOD'S WORD ABOUT GOD'S GUIDANCE

The Lord says, "I will make you wise and show you where to go. I will guide you and watch over you."

Psalm 32:8 NCV

The true children of God are those who let God's Spirit lead them.

Romans 8:14 NCV

Lord, You light my lamp; my God illuminates my darkness.

Psalm 18:28 HCSB

In all your ways acknowledge Him, and He shall direct your paths.

Proverbs 3:6 NKJV

Every morning he wakes me. He teaches me to listen like a student. The Lord God helps me learn . . .

Isaiah 50:4-5 NCV

MORE FOOD FOR THOUGHT ABOUT GOD'S GUIDANCE

It's incredible to realize that what we do each day has meaning in the big picture of God's plan.

Bill Hybels

God has a plan for the life of every Christian. Every circumstance, every turn of destiny, all things work together for your good and for His glory.

Billy Graham

If not a sparrow falls upon the ground without your Father, you have reason to see that the smallest events of your career and your life are arranged by him.

C. H. Spurgeon

If you believe in a God who controls the big things, you have to believe in a God who controls the little things. It is we, of course, to whom things look "little" or "big."

Elisabeth Elliot

God's goal is not to make you happy. It is to make you his.

Max Lucado

God has a course mapped out for your life, and all the inadequacies in the world will not change His mind. He will be with you every step of the way. And though it may take time, He has a celebration planned for when you cross over the "Red Seas" of your life.

Charles Swindoll

Our heavenly Father never takes anything from his children unless he means to give them something better.

George Mueller

I thought God's purpose was to make me full of happiness and joy. It is, but it is happiness and joy from God's standpoint, not from mine.

Oswald Chambers

I don't doubt that the Holy Spirit guides your decisions from within when you make them with the intention of pleasing God. The error would be to think that He speaks only within, whereas in reality He speaks also through Scripture, the Church, Christian friends, and books.

C. S. Lewis

POINTS OF EMPHASIS:
WRITE DOWN AT LEAST THREE THINGS THAT YOUR SON NEEDS TO HEAR FROM YOU ABOUT GOD'S GUIDANCE

2

Talk to Your Son About

Faith

DEAR SON, WITH FAITH, YOU CAN MOVE MOUNTAINS, WITHOUT FAITH, YOU CAN'T.

I assure you: If anyone says to this mountain, "Be lifted up and thrown into the sea," and does not doubt in his heart, but believes that what he says will happen, it will be done for him.

Mark 11:23 HCSB

Because we live in a demanding world, all of us, parents and children alike, have mountains to climb and mountains to move. Moving those mountains requires faith. And the experience of trying, with God's help, to move mountains builds character.

Faith, like a tender seedling, can be nurtured or neglected. When we nurture our faith through prayer, meditation, and worship, God blesses our lives and lifts our spirits. But when we fail to consult the Father early and often, we do ourselves and our loved ones a profound disservice.

Are you a mountain-moving person whose faith is evident for your son to see? Or, are you a spiritual shrinking violet? As you think about the answer to that question, consider this: God needs more people—and especially more parents—who are willing to move mountains for His glory and for His kingdom.

Every life—including your son's life—is a series of wins and losses. Every step of the way, through every triumph and every trial, God walks with your child, ready and willing to strengthen him. So the next time your son's character is being tested, remind him to take his concerns to God. And while you're at it, remind your youngster that no problem is too big for the Creator of the universe.

With God, all things are possible, and He stands ready to open a world of possibilities to your son and to you . . . if you have faith.

If you do not stand firm in your faith, then you will not stand at all.

Isaiah 7:9 HCSB

Be alert, stand firm in the faith, be brave and strong.

1 Corinthians 16:13 HCSB

For we walk by faith, not by sight.

2 Corinthians 5:7 HCSB

Now faith is the reality of what is hoped for, the proof of what is not seen.

Hebrews 11:1 HCSB

Now without faith it is impossible to please God, for the one who draws near to Him must believe that He exists and rewards those who seek Him.

Hebrews 11:6 HCSB

MORE FROM GOD'S WORD ABOUT FAITH AND WORSHIP

And every day they devoted themselves to meeting together in the temple complex, and broke bread from house to house. They ate their food with gladness and simplicity of heart, praising God and having favor with all the people. And every day the Lord added those being saved to them.

Acts 2:46-47 HCSB

But an hour is coming, and is now here, when the true worshipers will worship the Father in spirit and truth. Yes, the Father wants such people to worship Him. God is Spirit, and those who worship Him must worship in spirit and truth."

John 4:23-24 HCSB

For where two or three are gathered together in My name, I am there among them.

Matthew 18:20 HCSB

So that at the name of Jesus every knee should bow—of those who are in heaven and on earth and under the earth—and every tongue should confess that Jesus Christ is Lord, to the glory of God the Father.

Philippians 2:10-11 HCSB

MORE FOOD FOR THOUGHT ABOUT FAITH AND WORSHIP

There are a lot of things in life that are difficult to understand. Faith allows the soul to go beyond what the eyes can see.

John Maxwell

The popular idea of faith is of a certain obstinate optimism: the hope, tenaciously held in the face of trouble, that the universe is fundamentally friendly and things may get better.

J. I. Packer

I am truly grateful that faith enables me to move past the question of "Why?"

Zig Ziglar

When you enroll in the "school of faith," you never know what may happen next. The life of faith presents challenges that keep you going—and keep you growing!

Warren Wiersbe

Nothing is more disastrous than to study faith, analyze faith, make noble resolves of faith, but never actually to make the leap of faith.

Vance Havner

Faith is to believe what you do not see; the reward of this faith is to see what you believe.

St. Augustine

Faith's wings are clipped by reason's scissors.

R. G. Lee

Faith is nothing more or less than actively trusting God.

Catherine Marshall

Faith is trusting in advance what will only make sense in reverse.

Philip Yancey

POINTS OF EMPHASIS: WRITE DOWN AT LEAST THREE THINGS THAT YOUR SON NEEDS TO HEAR FROM YOU ABOUT FAITH

3

Talk to Your Son About
Doing What's Right

Dear Son, It's More Important to Be Right Than to Be Popular.

But run away from the evil young people like to do. Try hard to live right and to have faith, love, and peace, together with those who trust in the Lord from pure hearts.

2 Timothy 2:22 NCV

If your son is like most young men, he will seek the admiration of his friends and classmates. But the eagerness to please others should never overshadow his eagerness to please God. God has big plans for your son, and if your youngster intends to fulfill God's plans by following God's Son, then your son must seek to please the Father first and always.

Everyday life is an adventure in decision-making. Each day, your youngster will make countless decisions that will hopefully bring him closer to God. When your son obeys God's commandments, he inevitably experiences God's abundance and His peace. But, if your youngster turns his back on God by disobeying Him, your youngster will unintentionally invite Old Man Trouble to stop by for an extended visit.

Do you want your child to be successful and happy? Then encourage him to study God's Word and live by it.

If your son follows that advice, then when he faces a difficult choice or a powerful temptation (which he most certainly will), he'll be prepared to meet the enemy head-on.

So, as a thoughtful parent, your task is straightforward: encourage your child to seek God's approval in every aspect of his life. Does this sound too simple? Perhaps it is simple, but it is also the only way for your youngster to reap the marvelous riches that God has in store for him.

For the eyes of the Lord are over the righteous, and his ears are open unto their prayers: but the face of the Lord is against them that do evil.

1 Peter 3:12 KJV

Blessed are the pure of heart, for they will see God.

Matthew 5:8 NIV

But seek first his kingdom and his righteousness, and all these things will be given to you as well.

Matthew 6:33 NIV

The Lord will not reject his people; he will not abandon his own special possession. Judgement will come again for the righteous, and those who are upright will have a reward.

Psalm 94:14-15 NLT

The righteous shall flourish like the palm tree: he shall grow like a cedar in Lebanon.

Psalm 92:12 KJV

MORE FROM GOD'S WORD ABOUT OBEDIENCE TO GOD

Therefore, as we have opportunity, we must work for the good of all, especially for those who belong to the household of faith.

Galatians 6:10 HCSB

Make the most of every opportunity.

Colossians 4:5 NIV

Let us not lose heart in doing good, for in due time we shall reap if we do not grow weary. So then, while we have opportunity, let us do good to all men, and especially to those who are of the household of the faith.

Galatians 6:9-10 NASB

Dear brothers and sisters, whenever trouble comes your way, let it be an opportunity for joy. For when your faith is tested, your endurance has a chance to grow. So let it grow, for when your endurance is fully developed, you will be strong in character and ready for anything.

James 1:2-4 NLT

Remember ye not the former things, neither consider the things of old. Behold, I will do a new thing . . . .

Isaiah 43:18-19 KJV

MORE FOOD FOR THOUGHT ABOUT OBEDIENCE TO GOD

Impurity is not just a wrong action; impurity is the state of mind and heart and soul which is just the opposite of purity and wholeness.

A. W. Tozer

Righteousness not only defines God, but God defines righteousness.

Bill Hybels

Have your heart right with Christ, and he will visit you often, and so turn weekdays into Sundays, meals into sacraments, homes into temples, and earth into heaven.

C. H. Spurgeon

The great thing is to be found at one's post as a child of God, living each day as though it were our last, but planning as though our world might last a hundred years.

C. S. Lewis

What is God looking for? He is looking for men and women whose hearts are completely His.

Charles Swindoll

Learning God's truth and getting it into our heads is one thing, but living God's truth and getting it into our characters is quite something else.

Warren Wiersbe

Holiness is not the way to Jesus—Jesus is the way to holiness.

Anonymous

Many of the difficulties that we experience as Christians can be traced to a lack of Bible study. We should not be content to skim the Bible. We must place the Word of God in our hearts!

Billy Graham

Nobody is good by accident. No man ever became holy by chance.

C. H. Spurgeon

POINTS OF EMPHASIS:
WRITE DOWN AT LEAST THREE THINGS THAT YOUR SON NEEDS TO HEAR FROM YOU ABOUT OBEDIENCE TO GOD

4

Talk to Your Son About

Work

Dear Son, Hard Work Pays Tremendous Dividends, So the Time to Get Busy Is Now.

We must do the works of Him who sent Me while it is day. Night is coming when no one can work.

John 9:4 HCSB

Has your son acquired the habit of doing first things first, or is he one of those youngsters who put off important work until the last minute? The answer to this simple question will help determine how well he does in school, how quickly he succeeds in the workplace, and how much satisfaction he derives along the way.

God's Word teaches the value of hard work. In his second letter to the Thessalonians, Paul warns, ". . . if any would not work, neither should he eat" (3:10 KJV). And the Book of Proverbs proclaims, "One who is slack in his work is brother to one who destroys" (18:9 NIV). In short, God has created a world in which diligence is rewarded and laziness is not. And as a parent, it's up to you to convey this message to your son using both words and example (with a decided emphasis on the latter).

Your son will undoubtedly have countless opportunities to accomplish great things—but he should not expect life's greatest rewards to be delivered on a silver platter. Instead, he should pray as if everything depended upon God, but work as if everything depended upon himself. When he does, he can expect very big payoffs indeed.

Whatever you do, do it enthusiastically, as something done for the Lord and not for men.

Colossians 3:23 HCSB

Whatever your hands find to do, do with [all] your strength.

Ecclesiastes 9:10 HCSB

He did it with all his heart. So he prospered.

2 Chronicles 31:21 NKJV

Don't work only while being watched, in order to please men, but as slaves of Christ, do God's will from your heart. Render service with a good attitude, as to the Lord and not to men.

Ephesians 6:6-7 HCSB

We must do the works of Him who sent Me while it is day. Night is coming when no one can work.

John 9:4 HCSB

MORE FROM GOD'S WORD ABOUT SUCCESS

Success, success to you, and success to those who help you, for your God will help you . . . .

1 Chronicles 12:18 NIV

But as for you, be strong and do not give up, for your work will be rewarded.

2 Chronicles 15:7 NIV

Let us not become weary in doing good, for at the proper time we will reap a harvest if we do not give up.

Galatians 6:9 NIV

You need to persevere so that when you have done the will of God, you will receive what he has promised.

Hebrews 10:36 NIV

The one who understands a matter finds success, and the one who trusts in the Lord will be happy.

Proverbs 16:20 HCSB

MORE FOOD FOR THOUGHT ABOUT SUCCESS

We must trust as if it all depended on God and work as if it all depended on us.

C. H. Spurgeon

Thank God every morning when you get up that you have something which must be done, whether you like it or not. Work breeds a hundred virtues that idleness never knows.

Charles Kingsley

It may be that the day of judgment will dawn tomorrow; in that case, we shall gladly stop working for a better tomorrow. But not before.

Dietrich Bonhoeffer

Few things fire up a person's commitment like dedication to excellence.

John Maxwell

The world does not consider labor a blessing, therefore it flees and hates it, but the pious who fear the Lord labor with a ready and cheerful heart, for they know God's command, and they acknowledge His calling.

Martin Luther

I seem to have been led, little by little, toward my work; and I believe that the same fact will appear in the life of anyone who will cultivate such powers as God has given him and then go on, bravely, quietly, but persistently, doing such work as comes to his hands.

Fanny Crosby

Freedom is not an absence of responsibility; but rather a reward we receive when we've performed our responsibility with excellence.

Charles Swindoll

He will clothe you in rags if you clothe yourself with idleness.

C. H. Spurgeon

If, in your working hours, you make the work your end, you will presently find yourself all unawares inside the only circle in your profession that really matters. You will be one of the sound craftsmen, and other sound craftsmen will know it.

C. S. Lewis

Points of Emphasis:
Write Down at least Three Things That Your Son Needs to Hear from You About Success

5

Talk to Your Son About
Time Management

DEAR SON, LIFE IS SHORTER THAN YOU THINK, SO MAKE EVERY DAY COUNT.

So teach us to number our days,
that we may gain a heart of wisdom.

Psalm 90:12 NKJV

Time is a nonrenewable gift from God. But sometimes, all of us—both parents and children alike—treat our time here on earth as if it were not a gift at all: We may be tempted to invest our lives in trivial pursuits and petty diversions. Instead of doing what needs to be done now, we procrastinate. Yet our Father beckons each of us to a higher calling.

If you intend to be a responsible parent, you must teach your son to use time responsibly. After all, each waking moment holds the potential to do a good deed, to say a kind word, to fulfill a personal responsibility, or to offer a heartfelt prayer.

Time is a perishable commodity: we must use it or lose it. So your child's challenge (and yours) is to use the gift of time wisely. To do any less is an affront to the Creator and a prescription for disappointment.

Therefore, get your minds ready for action, being self-disciplined, and set your hope completely on the grace to be brought to you at the revelation of Jesus Christ.

1 Peter 1:13 HCSB

When you make a vow to God, don't delay fulfilling it, because He does not delight in fools. Fulfill what you vow.

Ecclesiastes 5:4 HCSB

If you do nothing in a difficult time, your strength is limited.

Proverbs 24:10 HCSB

Working together with Him, we also appeal to you: "Don't receive God's grace in vain." For He says: In an acceptable time, I heard you, and in the day of salvation, I helped you. Look, now is the acceptable time; look, now is the day of salvation.

2 Corinthians 6:1-2 HCSB

Be strong and courageous, and do the work. Don't be afraid or discouraged, for the Lord God, my God, is with you. He won't leave you or forsake you.

1 Chronicles 28:20 HCSB

MORE FOOD FOR THOUGHT ABOUT TIME MANAGEMENT

The more time you give to something, the more you reveal its importance and value to you.

Rick Warren

Our leisure, even our play, is a matter of serious concern. There is no neutral ground in the universe: every square inch, every split second, is claimed by God and counterclaimed by Satan.

C. S. Lewis

Stay busy. Get proper exercise. Eat the right foods. Don't spend time watching TV, lying in bed, or napping all day.

Truett Cathy

The work of God is appointed. There is always enough time to do the will of God.

Elisabeth Elliot

Our time is short! The time we can invest for God, in creative things, in receiving our fellowmen for Christ, is short!

Billy Graham

To choose time is to save time.

Francis Bacon

As we surrender the use of our time to the lordship of Christ, He will lead us to use it in the most productive way imaginable.

Charles Stanley

Frustration is not the will of God. There is time to do anything and everything that God wants us to do.

Elisabeth Elliot

Time here on earth is limited . . . use it or lose it!

Anonymous

Points of Emphasis:
Write Down at least Three Things That Your Son Needs to Hear from You About Time Management

6

Talk to Your Son About

Optimism

Dear Son, Optimism Pays, Pessimism Doesn't.

But if we look forward to something we don't have yet,
we must wait patiently and confidently.

Romans 8:25 NLT

Are you an optimistic, hopeful, enthusiastic Christian? You should be. After all, as a believer, you have every reason to be optimistic about life here on earth and life eternal. As English clergyman William Ralph Inge observed, "No Christian should be a pessimist, for Christianity is a system of radical optimism." Inge's words are most certainly true, but sometimes, you and your loved ones may find yourselves pulled down by the inevitable demands and worries of life here on earth. If so, it's time to ask yourself this question: what's bothering you, and why?

If you're worried by the inevitable challenges of everyday living, God wants to have a little talk with you. After all, the ultimate battle has already been won on the cross at Calvary. And if your life has been transformed by Christ's sacrifice, then you, as a recipient of God's grace, have every reason to live courageously.

Are you willing to trust God's plans for your life, and will you encourage your son to do the same? Hopefully so because even when the challenges of the day seem daunting, God remains steadfast. And, so should you.

So make this promise to yourself and keep it—vow to be a hope-filled parent. Think optimistically about your life, your profession, your family, your future, and your purpose for living. Trust your hopes, not your fears. Take time to celebrate God's glorious creation. And then, when you've filled your heart with hope and gladness, share your optimism with every member of your family. They'll be better for it, and so will you.

Make me hear joy and gladness.

Psalm 51:8 NKJV

For God has not given us a spirit of fearfulness, but one of power, love, and sound judgment.

2 Timothy 1:7 HCSB

My cup runs over. Surely goodness and mercy shall follow me all the days of my life; and I will dwell in the house of the Lord Forever.

Psalm 23:5-6 NKJV

I am able to do all things through Him who strengthens me.

Philippians 4:13 HCSB

Lord, I turn my hope to You. My God, I trust in You.

Psalm 25:1-2 HCSB

MORE FOOD FOR THOUGHT ABOUT OPTIMISM

It is a remarkable thing that some of the most optimistic and enthusiastic people you will meet are those who have been through intense suffering.

Warren Wiersbe

The popular idea of faith is of a certain obstinate optimism: the hope, tenaciously held in the face of trouble, that the universe is fundamentally friendly and things may get better.

J. I. Packer

Developing a positive attitude means working continually to find what is uplifting and encouraging.

Barbara Johnson

The essence of optimism is that it takes no account of the present, but it is a source of inspiration, of vitality, and of hope. Where others have resigned, it enables a man to hold his head high, to claim the future for himself, and not abandon it to his enemy.

Dietrich Bonhoeffer

Christ can put a spring in your step and a thrill in your heart. Optimism and cheerfulness are products of knowing Christ.

Billy Graham

The people whom I have seen succeed best in life have always been cheerful and hopeful people who went about their business with a smile on their faces.

Charles Kingsley

Keep your feet on the ground, but let your heart soar as high as it will. Refuse to be average or to surrender to the chill of your spiritual environment.

A. W. Tozer

If our hearts have been attuned to God through an abiding faith in Christ, the result will be joyous optimism and good cheer.

Billy Graham

The Christian lifestyle is not one of legalistic do's and don'ts, but one that is positive, attractive, and joyful.

Vonette Bright

Points of Emphasis:
Write Down at least Three Things That Your Son Needs to Hear from You About Optimism

7

Talk to Your Son About
Opportunity

Dear Son, Opportunities Are Everywhere, So Keep Your Eyes and Your Heart Open.

Therefore, as we have opportunity,
we must work for the good of all, especially for those who belong to the household of faith.

Galatians 6:10 HCSB

Because we are saved by a risen Christ, we can have hope for the future, no matter how troublesome our present circumstances may seem. After all, God has promised that we are His throughout eternity. And, He has told us that we must place our trust in Him.

Of course, we will face disappointments and failures while we are here on earth, but these are only temporary defeats. Of course, this world can be a place of trials and tribulations, but when we place our trust in the Giver of all things good, we are secure. God has promised us peace, joy, and eternal life. And God keeps His promises.

Whether you realize it or not, opportunities are whirling around you and your family like stars crossing the night sky: beautiful to observe, but too numerous to count. Yet you may be too concerned with the challenges of everyday living to notice those opportunities. That's why you should slow down occasionally, catch your breath, and focus your thoughts on two things: the talents and the opportunities that God has placed before you and your loved ones. God is leading you and your family in the direction of those opportunities. Your task is to watch carefully, to pray fervently, and to act accordingly.

You will show me the path of life; in Your presence is fullness of joy; at Your right hand are pleasures forevermore.

Psalm 16:11 NKJV

For I know the thoughts that I think toward you, says the Lord, thoughts of peace and not of evil, to give you a future and a hope. Then you will call upon Me and go and pray to Me, and I will listen to you.

Jeremiah 29:11-12 NKJV

But Jesus looked at them and said, "With men this is impossible, but with God all things are possible."

Matthew 19:26 HCSB

I am able to do all things through Him who strengthens me.

Philippians 4:13 HCSB

MORE FOOD FOR THOUGHT ABOUT OPPORTUNITY

Life is a glorious opportunity.

Billy Graham

We are all faced with a series of great opportunities, brilliantly disguised as unsolvable problems. Unsolvable without God's wisdom, that is.

Charles Swindoll

God has given you a unique set of talents and opportunities—talents and opportunities that can be built up or buried—and the choice to build or bury is entirely up to you.

Criswell Freeman

There is no limit to what God can make us—if we are willing.

Oswald Chambers

A wise man makes more opportunities than he finds.

Francis Bacon

With the right attitude and a willingness to pay the price, almost anyone can pursue nearly any opportunity and achieve it.

John Maxwell

He who waits until circumstances completely favor his undertaking will never accomplish anything.

Martin Luther

Every day we live is a priceless gift of God, loaded with possibilities to learn something new, to gain fresh insights.

Dale Evans Rogers

Great opportunities often disguise themselves in small tasks.

Rick Warren

Points of Emphasis:
Write Down at least Three Things That Your Son Needs to Hear from You About Opportunity

8

Talk to Your Son About

Safety

Dear Son, It's More Dangerous Out There Than You Think, So Play It Safe and Don't Be Impulsive.

The sensible see danger and take cover;
the foolish keep going and are punished.
Proverbs 27:12 HCSB

It's a nightmare that, from time to time, crosses the mind of every loving parent: the thought that serious injury might befall a child. These parental fears are reinforced by tragic accidents that, all too often, are splashed across the headlines of our local newspapers.

Since no one can deny that far too many young people behave recklessly, it's your job, as a responsible parent, to do everything within your power to ensure that your child is far more safety conscious than the norm. In short, you should become your family's safety advisor. You should be vocal, you should be persistent, you should be consistent, and you should be informed.

Maturity and safety go hand in hand. So, as your son becomes a more mature young man, he'll naturally, if gradually, acquire the habit of looking before he leaps. And that's good because when young people leap first and look second, they often engage in destructive behavior that they soon come to regret.

So don't hesitate to talk to your son about safety, don't hesitate to teach him safe behavior, don't hesitate to plan for his safety, and, when necessary, don't hesitate to limit his access to people and places that might cause him physical, emotional, or spiritual harm.

Being a strict, safety-conscious parent may not be the quickest path to parental popularity. But it's one of the best things you can do to help your son enjoy a long, happy, productive life.

Grow a wise heart—you'll do yourself a favor; keep a clear head—you'll find a good life.

Proverbs 19:8 MSG

Follow my advice, my son; always treasure my commands. Obey them and live! Guard my teachings as your most precious possession. Tie them on your fingers as a reminder. Write them deep within your heart.

Proverbs 7:1-3 NLT

Enthusiasm without knowledge is not good. If you act too quickly, you might make a mistake.

Proverbs 19:2 NCV

Therefore, everyone who hears these words of Mine and acts on them will be like a sensible man who built his house on the rock. The rain fell, the rivers rose, and the winds blew and pounded that house. Yet it didn't collapse, because its foundation was on the rock.

Matthew 7:24-25 HCSB

MORE FOOD FOR THOUGHT ABOUT SAFETY

Sometimes, being wise is nothing more than slowing down long enough to think about things before you do them.

Jim Gallery

If we neglect the Bible, we cannot expect to benefit from the wisdom and direction that result from knowing God's Word.

Vonette Bright

Knowledge can be found in books or in school. Wisdom, on the other hand, starts with God . . . and ends there.

Marie T. Freeman

This is my song through endless ages: Jesus led me all the way.

Fanny Crosby

Wisdom is knowledge applied. Head knowledge is useless on the battlefield. Knowledge stamped on the heart makes one wise.

Beth Moore

When you and I are related to Jesus Christ, our strength and wisdom and peace and joy and love and hope may run out, but His life rushes in to keep us filled to the brim. We are showered with blessings, not because of anything we have or have not done, but simply because of Him.

Anne Graham Lotz

Patience is the companion of wisdom.

St. Augustine

The more wisdom enters our hearts, the more we will be able to trust our hearts in difficult situations.

John Eldredge

Points of Emphasis:
Write Down at least Three Things That Your Son Needs to Hear from You About Safety

9

Talk to Your Son About

Character

Dear Son, The Sooner You Learn That Character Really Matters, the Sooner You'll Earn the Respect of Your Peers and Yourself.

People with integrity have firm footing,
but those who follow crooked paths will slip and fall.

Proverbs 10:9 NLT

It has been said that character is what we are when nobody is watching. How true. When we do things that we know aren't right, we try to hide them from our families and friends. But even if we successfully conceal our sins from the world, we can never conceal our sins from God.

Charles Swindoll correctly observed, "Nothing speaks louder or more powerfully than a life of integrity." Wise parents agree.

Integrity is built slowly over a lifetime. It is the sum of every right decision and every honest word. It is forged on the anvil of honorable work and polished by the twin virtues of honesty and fairness. Integrity is a precious thing—difficult to build but easy to tear down.

Living a life of integrity isn't always the easiest way, especially for a young person like your son. After all, he inhabits a world that presents him with countless temptations to stray far from God's path. So as a parent, your job is to remind him (again and again) that whenever he's confronted with sin, he should walk—or better yet run—in the opposite direction. And the good news is this: When your son makes up his mind to walk with Jesus every day, his character will take care of itself . . . and he won't need to look over his shoulder to see who, besides God, is watching.

As the water reflects the face, so the heart reflects the person.

Proverbs 27:19 HCSB

We also rejoice in our afflictions, because we know that affliction produces endurance, endurance produces proven character, and proven character produces hope.

Romans 5:3-4 HCSB

A good name is to be chosen rather than great riches, loving favor rather than silver and gold.

Proverbs 22:1 NKJV

Do not be deceived: "Evil company corrupts good habits."

1 Corinthians 15:33 NKJV

In all things showing yourself to be a pattern of good works; in doctrine showing integrity, reverence, incorruptibility . . . .

Titus 2:7 NKJV

MORE FROM GOD'S WORD ABOUT CHARACTER

For everyone who practices wicked things hates the light and avoids it, so that his deeds may not be exposed. But anyone who lives by the truth comes to the light, so that his works may be shown to be accomplished by God.

John 3:20–21 HCSB

Be diligent to present yourself approved to God, a worker who doesn't need to be ashamed, correctly teaching the word of truth.

2 Timothy 2:15 HCSB

I have no greater joy than this: to hear that my children are walking in the truth.

3 John 1:4 HCSB

When the Spirit of truth comes, He will guide you into all the truth.

John 16:13 HCSB

You will know the truth, and the truth will set you free.

John 8:32 HCSB

MORE FOOD FOR THOUGHT ABOUT CHARACTER

There is something about having endured great loss that brings purity of purpose and strength of character.

Barbara Johnson

Often, our character is at greater risk in prosperity than in adversity.

Beth Moore

We actually are, at present, creatures whose character must be, in some respects, a horror to God, as it is, when we really see it, a horror to ourselves. This I believe to be a fact: and I notice that the holier a man is, the more fully he is aware of that fact.

C. S. Lewis

Each one of us is God's special work of art. Through us, He teaches and inspires, delights and encourages, informs and uplifts all those who view our lives. God, the master artist, is most concerned about expressing Himself—His thoughts and His intentions—through what He paints in our characters.

Joni Eareckson Tada

Integrity is the glue that holds our way of life together. We must constantly strive to keep our integrity intact. When wealth is lost, nothing is lost; when health is lost, something is lost; when character is lost, all is lost.

Billy Graham

Integrity is not a given factor in everyone's life. It is a result of self-discipline, inner trust, and a decision to be relentlessly honest in all situations in our lives.

John Maxwell

Honesty has a beautiful and refreshing simplicity about it. No ulterior motives. No hidden meanings. As honesty and integrity characterize our lives, there will be no need to manipulate others.

Charles Swindoll

The single most important element in any human relationship is honesty—with oneself, with God, and with others.

Catherine Marshall

Sow an act, and you reap a habit. Sow a habit and you reap a character. Sow a character and you reap a destiny.

Anonymous

POINTS OF EMPHASIS:
WRITE DOWN AT LEAST THREE THINGS THAT YOUR SON NEEDS TO HEAR FROM YOU ABOUT CHARACTER

10

Talk to Your Son About

Celebrating Life the Right Way

DEAR SON, IF YOU DON'T CELEBRATE LIFE, NOBODY'S GOING TO CELEBRATE IT FOR YOU.

This is the day the Lord has made;
let us rejoice and be glad in it.

Psalm 118:24 HCSB

The 118th Psalm reminds us that today, like every other day, is a cause for celebration. God gives us this day; He fills it to the brim with possibilities, and He challenges us to use it for His purposes. The day is presented to us fresh and clean at midnight, free of charge, but we must beware: Today is a non-renewable resource—once it's gone, it's gone forever. Our responsibility, of course, is to use this day in the service of God's will and according to His commandments.

If your son is like most people, he may, at times, fall victim to the negativity and cynicism of our negative age. And if that happens, it's up to you to remind him that every day is a gift and that he should treasure the time that God has given him.

The Christian life should be a triumphal celebration, a daily exercise in thanksgiving and praise. Encourage your son to join that celebration. And while you're at it, make sure that you've joined in the celebration, too.

Celebrate God all day, every day. I mean, revel in him!

Philippians 4:4 MSG

David and the whole house of Israel were celebrating before the Lord.

2 Samuel 6:5 HCSB

Their sorrow was turned into rejoicing and their mourning into a holiday. They were to be days of feasting, rejoicing, and of sending gifts to one another and the poor.

Esther 9:22 HCSB

At the dedication of the wall of Jerusalem, they sent for the Levites wherever they lived and brought them to Jerusalem to celebrate the joyous dedication with thanksgiving and singing accompanied by cymbals, harps, and lyres.

Nehemiah 12:27 HCSB

These things I have spoken to you, that My joy may remain in you, and that your joy may be full.

John 15:11 NKJV

MORE FROM GOD'S WORD ABOUT CHEERFULNESS

Be cheerful. Keep things in good repair. Keep your spirits up. Think in harmony. Be agreeable. Do all that, and the God of love and peace will be with you for sure.

2 Corinthians 13:11 MSG

Jacob said, "For what a relief it is to see your friendly smile. It is like seeing the smile of God!"

Genesis 33:10 NLT

Do everything readily and cheerfully—no bickering, no second-guessing allowed! Go out into the world uncorrupted, a breath of fresh air in this squalid and polluted society. Provide people with a glimpse of good living and of the living God. Carry the light-giving Message into the night.

Philippians 2:14-15 MSG

Is anyone happy? Let him sing songs of praise

James 5:13 NIV

God loves a cheerful giver.

2 Corinthians 9:7 NIV

MORE FOOD FOR THOUGHT ABOUT CHEERFULNESS

Joy is the direct result of having God's perspective on our daily lives and the effect of loving our Lord enough to obey His commands and trust His promises.

Bill Bright

Our sense of joy, satisfaction, and fulfillment in life increases, no matter what the circumstances, if we are in the center of God's will.

Billy Graham

When we get rid of inner conflicts and wrong attitudes toward life, we will almost automatically burst into joy.

E. Stanley Jones

Some of us seem so anxious about avoiding hell that we forget to celebrate our journey toward heaven.

Philip Yancey

In the absence of all other joys, the joy of the Lord can fill the soul to the brim.

C. H. Spurgeon

God knows everything. He can manage everything, and He loves us. Surely this is enough for a fullness of joy that is beyond words.

Hannah Whitall Smith

A life of intimacy with God is characterized by joy.

Oswald Chambers

True happiness and contentment cannot come from the things of this world. The blessedness of true joy is a free gift that comes only from our Lord and Savior, Jesus Christ.

Dennis Swanberg

Joy is the serious business of heaven.

C. S. Lewis

Points of Emphasis:
Write Down at least Three Things That Your Son Needs to Hear from You About Cheerfulness

11

Talk to Your Son About

Regret

DEAR SON, YOU CAN'T WIN THEM ALL; DON'T WASTE TIME REGRETTING THE ONES YOU LOSE.

One thing I do, forgetting those things which are behind and reaching forward to those things which are ahead, I press toward the goal for the prize of the upward call of God in Christ Jesus.

Philippians 3:13-14 NKJV

As the old saying goes, "You win some, and you lose some." It's a simple lesson, but probably a tough lesson for your son to learn. After all, your youngster inhabits a society that glorifies winners and minimizes losers. So when your boy wins, he's encouraged—at least by a growing collection of chest-thumping sports icons—to engage in wild, in-your-face celebrations. And when he loses, he's encouraged—at least on a subconscious level—to consider himself "a loser." Yet nothing could be further from the truth. Real success has little to do with the temporary wins and losses of everyday life. Real victory comes when we choose to trust God's Word and follow God's Son.

If your son is bitter about some past defeat, you should remind him that bitterness is a spiritual sickness, a potentially destructive emotion that can rob him of happiness and peace.

So how can your son rid himself of regret? First, he should prayerfully ask God to cleanse his heart. Then, he must learn to catch himself whenever feelings of anger or bitterness invade his thoughts. In short, he must learn to recognize and to resist negative thoughts before those thoughts hijack his emotions.

The great sports writer Grantland Rice wrote, "For when the one Great Scorer comes to write against your name, He marks not that you won or lost, but how you played the game." That's a message that your son needs to learn now—and if you're a savvy parent, you'll help him learn it. Now.

Do not remember the past events, pay no attention to things of old. Look, I am about to do something new; even now it is coming. Do you not see it? Indeed, I will make a way in the wilderness, rivers in the desert.

Isaiah 43:18-19 HCSB

Consider it a great joy, my brothers, whenever you experience various trials, knowing that the testing of your faith produces endurance. But endurance must do its complete work, so that you may be mature and complete, lacking nothing.

James 1:2-4 HCSB

I will thank you, Lord, with all my heart; I will tell of all the marvelous things you have done. I will be filled with joy because of you. I will sing praises to your name, O Most High.

Psalm 9:1-2 NLT

Now I am coming to You, and I speak these things in the world so that they may have My joy completed in them.

John 17:13 HCSB

MORE FOOD FOR THOUGHT ABOUT REGRET

Get rid of the poison of built-up anger and the acid of long-term resentment.

Charles Swindoll

Our yesterdays present irreparable things to us; it is true that we have lost opportunities which will never return, but God can transform this destructive anxiety into a constructive thoughtfulness for the future. Let the past sleep, but let it sleep on the bosom of Christ. Leave the Irreparable Past in His hands, and step out into the Irresistible Future with Him.

Oswald Chambers

In the Christian story God descends to reascend. He comes down; . . . down to the very roots and sea-bed of the Nature he has created. But He goes down to come up again and bring the whole ruined world with Him.

C. S. Lewis

There is no road back to yesterday.

Oswald Chambers

Sold for thirty pieces of silver, he redeemed the world.

R. G. Lee

For God is not merely mending, not simply restoring a status quo. Redeemed humanity is to be something more glorious than unfallen humanity.

C. S. Lewis

The enemy of our souls loves to taunt us with past failures, wrongs, disappointments, disasters, and calamities. And if we let him continue doing this, our life becomes a long and dark tunnel, with very little light at the end.

Charles Swindoll

Leave the broken, irreversible past in God's hands, and step out into the invincible future with Him.

Oswald Chambers

He is ever faithful and gives us the song in the night to soothe our spirits and fresh joy each morning to lift our souls. What a marvelous Lord!

Bill Bright

Points of Emphasis:
Write Down at least Three Things That Your Son Needs to Hear from You About Regret

12

Talk to Your Son About
Service

Dear Son, It's Important to Serve.

The greatest among you will be your servant.
Whoever exalts himself will be humbled,
and whoever humbles himself will be exalted.

Matthew 23:11-12 HCSB

If you and your family members genuinely seek to discover God's unfolding priorities for your lives, you must ask yourselves this question: "How does God want us to serve others?" And you may be certain of this: service to others is an integral part of God's plan for your lives, a plan that the Creator intends for you to impart to your son.

Christ was the ultimate servant, the Savior who gave His life for mankind. As His followers, we, too, must become humble servants. As Christians, we are clearly (and repeatedly) instructed to assist those in need. But, as weak human beings, we sometimes fall short as we seek to puff ourselves up and glorify our own accomplishments. Jesus commands otherwise. He teaches us that the most esteemed men and women are not the self-congratulatory leaders of society but are instead the humblest of servants.

Is your family willing to roll up its sleeves and become humble servants for Christ? Are you willing to do your part to make the world a better place? Are you willing to serve God now and trust Him to bless you later? The answer to these questions will determine the direction of your lives and the quality of your service.

As members of God's family, we must serve our neighbors quietly and without fanfare. We must find needs and meet them. We must lend helping hands and share kind words with humility in our hearts and praise on our lips. And we must remember that every time we help someone in need, we are serving our Savior . . . which, by the way, is precisely what we must do.

Worship the Lord your God and . . . serve Him only.

Matthew 4:10 HCSB

A person should consider us in this way: as servants of Christ and managers of God's mysteries. In this regard, it is expected of managers that each one be found faithful.

1 Corinthians 4:1-2 HCSB

If they serve Him obediently, they will end their days in prosperity and their years in happiness.

Job 36:11 HCSB

Serve the Lord with gladness.

Psalm 100:2 HCSB

MORE FOOD FOR THOUGHT ABOUT SERVICE

Before the judgment seat of Christ, my service will not be judged by how much I have done but by how much of me there is in it.

A. W. Tozer

When you're enjoying the fulfillment and fellowship that inevitably accompanies authentic service, ministry is a joy. Instead of exhausting you, it energizes you; instead of burnout, you experience blessing.

Bill Hybels

No life can surpass that of a man who quietly continues to serve God in the place where providence has placed him.

C. H. Spurgeon

Make it a rule, and pray to God to help you to keep it, never, if possible, to lie down at night without being able to say: "I have made one human being at least a little wiser, or a little happier, or at least a little better this day."

Charles Kingsley

Opportunities for service abound, and you will be surprised that when you seek God's direction, a place of suitable service will emerge where you can express your love through service.

Charles Stanley

In God's family, there is to be one great body of people: servants. In fact, that's the way to the top in his kingdom.

Charles Swindoll

In Jesus, the service of God and the service of the least of the brethren were one.

Dietrich Bonhoeffer

You can judge how far you have risen in the scale of life by asking one question: How wisely and how deeply do I care? To be Christianized is to be sensitized. Christians are people who care.

E. Stanley Jones

Service is the pathway to real significance.

Rick Warren

Points of Emphasis: Write Down at least Three Things That Your Son Needs to Hear from You About Service

13

Talk to Your Son About
Humility

Dear Son, Since Pride Usually Precedes a Fall, Stay Humble.

Humble yourselves therefore under the mighty hand of God,
so that He may exalt you in due time,
casting all your care upon Him, because He cares about you.

1 Peter 5:6-7 HCSB

God's Word clearly instructs us to be humble. And that's good because, as fallible human beings, we have so very much to be humble about. Besides, God promises to bless the humble and correct the prideful. So why, then, are we humans so full of ourselves? The answer, of course, is that, if we are honest with ourselves and with our God, we simply can't be boastful; we should, instead, be eternally grateful and exceedingly humble. Yet humility is not, in most cases, a naturally occurring human trait.

Most of us, grownups and kids alike, are more than willing to overestimate our own accomplishments. We are tempted to say, "Look how wonderful I am!" . . . hoping all the while that the world will agree with our own self-appraisals. But those of us who fall prey to the sin of pride should beware—God is definitely not impressed by our prideful proclamations.

God honors humility . . . and He rewards those who humbly serve Him. So if you've acquired the wisdom to be humble, and if you're teaching your son to do likewise, you are to be congratulated. But if you've not yet overcome the tendency to overestimate your own accomplishments, or if your son seems overly impressed with his own accomplishments, then God still has some important (and perhaps painful) lessons to teach you—lessons about humility that you and your loved ones may still need to learn.

Clothe yourselves with humility toward one another, because God resists the proud, but gives grace to the humble.

1 Peter 5:5 HCSB

But He said to me, "My grace is sufficient for you, for power is perfected in weakness." Therefore, I will most gladly boast all the more about my weaknesses, so that Christ's power may reside in me.

2 Corinthians 12:9 HCSB

You will save the humble people; But Your eyes are on the haughty, that You may bring them down.

2 Samuel 22:28 NKJV

If My people who are called by My name will humble themselves, and pray and seek My face, and turn from their wicked ways, then I will hear from heaven, and will forgive their sin and heal their land.

2 Chronicles 7:14 NKJV

Do nothing out of rivalry or conceit, but in humility consider others as more important than yourselves.

Philippians 2:3 HCSB

More from God's Word About Giving God the Praise He Deserves

Praise the Lord, all nations! Glorify Him, all peoples! For great is His faithful love to us; the Lord's faithfulness endures forever. Hallelujah!

Psalm 117 HCSB

Therefore, through Him let us continually offer up to God a sacrifice of praise, that is, the fruit of our lips that confess His name.

Hebrews 13:15 HCSB

So that at the name of Jesus every knee should bow—of those who are in heaven and on earth and under the earth—and every tongue should confess that Jesus Christ is Lord, to the glory of God the Father.

Philippians 2:10-11 HCSB

Enter into his gates with thanksgiving, and into his courts with praise: be thankful unto him, and bless his name. For the LORD is good; his mercy is everlasting; and his truth endureth to all generations.

Psalm 100:4-5 KJV

MORE FOOD FOR THOUGHT ABOUT GIVING GOD THE PRAISE HE DESERVES

I can usually sense that a leading is from the Holy Spirit when it calls me to humble myself, to serve somebody, to encourage somebody, or to give something away. Very rarely will the evil one lead us to do those kind of things.

Bill Hybels

Because Christ Jesus came to the world clothed in humility, he will always be found among those who are clothed with humility. He will be found among the humble people.

A. W. Tozer

All kindness and good deeds, we must keep silent. The result will be an inner reservoir of personality power.

Catherine Marshall

One never can see, or not till long afterwards, why any one was selected for any job. And when one does, it is usually some reason that leaves no room for vanity.

C. S. Lewis

Let the love of Christ be believed in and felt in your hearts, and it will humble you.

C. H. Spurgeon

We are never stronger than the moment we admit we are weak.

Beth Moore

That some of my hymns have been dictated by the blessed Holy Spirit I have no doubt; and that others have been the result of deep meditation I know to be true; but that the poet has any right to claim special merit for himself is certainly presumptuous.

Fanny Crosby

Jesus had a humble heart. If He abides in us, pride will never dominate our lives.

Billy Graham

Faith itself cannot be strong where humility is weak.

C. H. Spurgeon

POINTS OF EMPHASIS:
WRITE DOWN AT LEAST THREE THINGS THAT YOUR SON NEEDS TO HEAR FROM YOU ABOUT BEING HUMBLE

14

Talk to Your Son About Kindness

Dear Son, It Pays to Be Respectful, So Treat Everybody Like You'd Want to Be Treated If You Were in Their Shoes.

Therefore, whatever you want others to do for you, do also the same for them—this is the Law and the Prophets.

Matthew 7:12 HCSB

All over the world, loving parents preach the same lesson: kindness. And Christ taught that very same lesson when He spoke the words recorded in Matthew 7:12.

The Bible instructs us to be courteous and compassionate—and God's Word promises that when we follow these instructions, we are blessed. But sometimes, we fall short. Sometimes, amid the busyness and confusion of everyday life, we may neglect to share a kind word or a kind deed. This oversight hurts others, and it hurts us as well.

The Golden Rule commands us to treat others as we wish to be treated. When we weave the thread of kindness into the very fabric of our lives, we give glory to the One who gave His life for us.

Your son is growing up in a cynical society that often seems to focus on self-gratification and self-centeredness. Yet God's Word warns against becoming too attached to the world, and it's a warning that applies both to your son and to you.

So today, slow yourself down and be alert for those who need a smile, a kind word, or a helping hand. And encourage your son to do the same—encourage him to make kindness a centerpiece of his dealings with others. When he does, he'll discover that life is simply better when he treats other people in the same way he would want to be treated if he were in their shoes.

Finally, all of you be of one mind, having compassion for one another; love as brothers, be tenderhearted, be courteous.

1 Peter 3:8 NKJV

Love is patient; love is kind.

1 Corinthians 13:4 HCSB

And may the Lord make you increase and abound in love to one another and to all.

1 Thessalonians 3:12 NKJV

And be kind and compassionate to one another, forgiving one another, just as God also forgave you in Christ.

Ephesians 4:32 HCSB

Pure and undefiled religion before our God and Father is this: to look after orphans and widows in their distress and to keep oneself unstained by the world.

James 1:27 HCSB

MORE FROM GOD'S WORD ABOUT GENEROSITY

Dear friend, you are showing your faith by whatever you do for the brothers, and this you are doing for strangers.

3 John 1:5 HCSB

In every way I've shown you that by laboring like this, it is necessary to help the weak and to keep in mind the words of the Lord Jesus, for He said, "It is more blessed to give than to receive."

Acts 20:35 HCSB

Bear one another's burdens, and so fulfill the law of Christ.

Galatians 6:2 NKJV

If a brother or sister is without clothes and lacks daily food, and one of you says to them, "Go in peace, keep warm, and eat well," but you don't give them what the body needs, what good is it?

James 2:15–16 HCSB

MORE FOOD FOR THOUGHT ABOUT GENEROSITY

The golden rule to follow to obtain spiritual understanding is not one of intellectual pursuit, but one of obedience.

Oswald Chambers

The #1 rule of friendship is the Golden one.

Criswell Freeman

Love is not grabbing, or self-centered, or selfish. Real love is being able to contribute to the happiness of another person without expecting to get anything in return.

James Dobson

Our lives, we are told, are but fleeting at best, / Like roses they fade and decay; / Then let us do good while the present is ours, / Be useful as long as we stay.

Fanny Crosby

When you extend hospitality to others, you're not trying to impress people, you're trying to reflect God to them.

Max Lucado

Faith never asks whether good works are to be done, but has done them before there is time to ask the question, and it is always doing them.

Martin Luther

We must mirror God's love in the midst of a world full of hatred. We are the mirrors of God's love, so we may show Jesus by our lives.

Corrie ten Boom

If we have the true love of God in our hearts, we will show it in our lives. We will not have to go up and down the earth proclaiming it. We will show it in everything we say or do.

D. L. Moody

Be so preoccupied with good will that you haven't room for ill will.

E. Stanley Jones

POINTS OF EMPHASIS:
WRITE DOWN AT LEAST THREE THINGS THAT YOUR SON NEEDS TO HEAR FROM YOU ABOUT GENEROSITY

15

Talk to Your Son About

Lifetime Learning

Dear Son, You're Never Too Old (or Too Young) to Learn Something New.

Apply yourself to instruction and listen to words of knowledge.

Proverbs 23:12 HCSB

As long as we live, we should continue to learn, and we should encourage our children to do likewise. But sometimes the job of teaching our kids seems to be a thankless one. Why? Because sometimes our children pay scant attention to the educational opportunities that we adults work so hard to provide for them.

Education is the tool by which all of us—parents and children alike—come to know and appreciate the world in which we live. It is the shining light that snuffs out the darkness of ignorance and poverty. Education is freedom just as surely as ignorance is a form of bondage. Education is not a luxury; it is a necessity and a powerful tool for good in this world.

When it comes to learning life's most important lessons, we can either do things the easy way or the hard way. The easy way can be summed up as follows: when God teaches us a lesson, we learn it . . . the first time. Unfortunately, too many of us learn much more slowly than that.

When we resist God's instruction, He continues to teach, whether we like it or not. Our challenge, then, is to discern God's lessons from the experiences of everyday life. Hopefully, we learn those lessons sooner rather than later because the sooner we do, the sooner He can move on to the next lesson and the next and the next.

So your challenge, as a thoughtful parent, is straightforward: to convince your son that he still has much to learn, even if your boy would prefer to believe otherwise.

If you listen to correction to improve your life, you will live among the wise.

Proverbs 15:31 NCV

A wise heart accepts commands, but foolish lips will be destroyed.

Proverbs 10:8 HCSB

The fear of the Lord is the beginning of knowledge, but fools despise wisdom and discipline.

Proverbs 1:7 NIV

The knowledge of the secrets of the kingdom of heaven has been given to you . . . .

Matthew 13:11 NIV

MORE FROM GOD'S WORD ABOUT MATURITY

But grow in grace, and in the knowledge of our Lord and Saviour Jesus Christ . . . .

2 Peter 3:18 KJV

Continue in what you have learned and have become convinced of, because you know those from whom you learned it, and how from infancy you have known the holy Scriptures, which are able to make you wise for salvation through faith in Christ Jesus.

2 Timothy 3:14, 15 NIV

Consider it pure joy, my brothers, whenever you face trials of many kinds, because you know that the testing of your faith develops perseverance. Perseverance must finish its work so that you may be mature and complete, not lacking anything.

James 1:2-4 NIV

You must follow the Lord your God and fear Him. You must keep His commands and listen to His voice; you must worship Him and remain faithful to Him.

Deuteronomy 13:4 HCSB

MORE FOOD FOR THOUGHT ABOUT MATURITY

The wonderful thing about God's schoolroom is that we get to grade our own papers. You see, He doesn't test us so He can learn how well we're doing. He tests us so we can discover how well we're doing.

Charles Swindoll

True learning can take place at every age of life, and it doesn't have to be in the curriculum plan.

Suzanne Dale Ezell

While chastening is always difficult, if we look to God for the lesson we should learn, we will see spiritual fruit.

Vonette Bright

The maturity of a Christian experience cannot be reached in a moment, but is the result of the work of God's Holy Spirit, who, by His energizing and transforming power, causes us to grow up into Christ in all things.

Hannah Whitall Smith

The wise man gives proper appreciation in his life to his past. He learns to sift the sawdust of heritage in order to find the nuggets that make the current moment have any meaning.

Grady Nutt

It's the things you learn after you know it all that really count.

Vance Havner

Our loving God uses difficulty in our lives to burn away the sin of self and build faith and spiritual power.

Bill Bright

I don't doubt that the Holy Spirit guides your decisions from within when you make them with the intention of pleasing God. The error would be to think that He speaks only within, whereas in reality He speaks also through Scripture, the Church, Christian friends, and books.

C. S. Lewis

POINTS OF EMPHASIS:
WRITE DOWN AT LEAST THREE THINGS THAT YOUR SON NEEDS TO HEAR FROM YOU ABOUT MATURITY

16

Talk to Your Son About
Responsibility

Dear Son, Don't Depend on Luck, and While You're at It, Don't Try to Get Something for Nothing.

Don't be deceived: God is not mocked. For whatever a man sows he will also reap, because the one who sows to his flesh will reap corruption from the flesh, but the one who sows to the Spirit will reap eternal life from the Spirit.

Galatians 6:7-8 HCSB

How hard is it for young people to act responsibly? Sometimes, when youngsters are beset by negative role models and unrelenting peer pressure, it can be very difficult for them to do the right thing. Difficult, but not impossible.

Nobody needs to tell your son the obvious: He has many responsibilities—obligations to himself, to his family, to his community, to his school, and to his Creator. And which of these duties should take priority? The answer can be found in Matthew 6:33: "But seek first the kingdom of God and His righteousness, and all these things will be provided for you" (HCSB).

When your son "seeks first the kingdom of God," all the other obligations have a way of falling into place. And when your son learns the importance of honoring God with his time, his talents, and his prayers, he'll be much more likely to behave responsibly.

So do your youngster a favor: encourage him to take all his duties seriously, especially his duties to God. If he follows your advice, your child will soon discover that pleasing his Father in heaven isn't just the right thing to do; it's also the best way to live.

But each person should examine his own work, and then he will have a reason for boasting in himself alone, and not in respect to someone else. For each person will have to carry his own load.

Galatians 6:4-5 HCSB

So then each of us shall give account of himself to God.

Romans 14:12 NKJV

"Therefore I will judge you, O house of Israel, every one according to his ways," says the Lord God.

Ezekiel 18:30 NKJV

We always pray for you that our God will consider you worthy of His calling, and will, by His power, fulfill every desire for goodness and the work of faith, so that the name of our Lord Jesus will be glorified by you, and you by Him, according to the grace of our God and the Lord Jesus Christ.

2 Thessalonians 1:11-12 HCSB

MORE FROM GOD'S WORD ABOUT DOING WHAT'S RIGHT

Therefore, get your minds ready for action, being self-disciplined, and set your hope completely on the grace to be brought to you at the revelation of Jesus Christ. As obedient children, do not be conformed to the desires of your former ignorance but, as the One who called you is holy, you also are to be holy in all your conduct.

1 Peter 1:13-15 HCSB

Lead a tranquil and quiet life in all godliness and dignity.

1 Timothy 2:2 HCSB

For this very reason, make every effort to supplement your faith with goodness, goodness with knowledge, knowledge with self-control, self-control with endurance, endurance with godliness.

2 Peter 1:5-6 HCSB

Be an example to the believers in word, in conduct, in love, in spirit, in faith, in purity.

1 Timothy 4:12 NKJV

More Food for Thought About Doing What's Right

Do not pray for easy lives. Pray to be stronger men! Do not pray for tasks equal to your powers. Pray for powers equal to your tasks.

Phillips Brooks

Whether we know it or not, whether we agree with it or not, whether we practice it or not, whether we like it or not, we are accountable to one another.

Charles Stanley

Although God causes all things to work together for good for His children, He still holds us accountable for our behavior.

Kay Arthur

God never does anything for a man that the man can do for himself. The Lord is too busy for that. So look after your own business and let the Good Lord look after His.

Sam Jones

Action springs not from thought, but from a readiness for responsibility.

Dietrich Bonhoeffer

Our trustworthiness implies His trustworthiness.

Beth Moore

Living life with a consistent spiritual walk deeply influences those we love most.

Vonette Bright

Hoping for a good future without investing in today is like a farmer waiting for a crop without ever planting any seed.

John Maxwell

To walk out of His will is to walk into nowhere.

C. S. Lewis

Points of Emphasis:
Write Down at least Three Things That Your Son Needs to Hear from You About Doing What's Right

17

Talk to Your Son About

Perseverance

Dear Son, It's Important to Know When Not to Give Up.

Though a righteous man falls seven times,
he will get up, but the wicked will stumble into ruin.

Proverbs 24:16 HCSB

As he makes his way through life, your son will undoubtedly experience his fair share of disappointments, detours, false starts, and failures. Whenever he encounters one of life's dead ends, he'll face a test of character. So the question of the day is not if your boy will be tested; it's how he will respond.

The old saying is as true today as it was when it was first spoken: "Life is a marathon, not a sprint." That's why wise travelers select a traveling companion who never tires and never falters. That partner, of course, is God.

The next time your son's courage is tested to the limit, remind him that God is always near and that the Creator offers strength and comfort to those who are wise enough to ask for it. Your son's job, of course, is to ask.

God operates on His own timetable, and sometimes He may answer your child's prayers with silence. But if your son remains steadfast, he may soon be surprised at the creative ways that God finds to help determined believers who possess the wisdom and the courage to persevere.

Let us not become weary in doing good, for at the proper time we will reap a harvest if we do not give up.

Galatians 6:9 NIV

For you have need of endurance, so that when you have done the will of God, you may receive what was promised.

Hebrews 10:36 NASB

Thanks be to God! He gives us the victory through our Lord Jesus Christ. Therefore, my dear brothers, stand firm. Let nothing move you. Always give yourselves fully to the work of the Lord, because you know that your labor in the Lord is not in vain.

1 Corinthians 15:57-58 NIV

Be diligent that ye may be found of him in peace, without spot, and blameless.

2 Peter 3:14 KJV

It is better to finish something than to start it. It is better to be patient than to be proud.

Ecclesiastes 7:8 NCV

MORE FROM GOD'S WORD ABOUT PATIENCE

We urge you, brethren, admonish the unruly, encourage the fainthearted, help the weak, be patient with everyone.

1 Thessalonians 5:14 NASB

Be completely humble and gentle; be patient, bearing with one another in love.

Ephesians 4:2 NIV

Wherefore seeing we also are compassed about with so great a cloud of witnesses, let us lay aside every weight, and the sin which doth so easily beset us, and let us run with patience the race that is set before us . . . .

Hebrews 12:1 KJV

Yet the LORD longs to be gracious to you; he rises to show you compassion. For the LORD is a God of justice. Blessed are all who wait for him!

Isaiah 30:18 NIV

Wait on the LORD; Be of good courage, and He shall strengthen your heart; Wait, I say, on the LORD!

Psalm 27:14 NKJV

MORE FOOD FOR THOUGHT ABOUT PATIENCE

Battles are won in the trenches, in the grit and grime of courageous determination; they are won day by day in the arena of life.

Charles Swindoll

You cannot persevere unless there is a trial in your life. There can be no victories without battles; there can be no peaks without valleys. If you want the blessing, you must be prepared to carry the burden and fight the battle. God has to balance privileges with responsibilities, blessings with burdens, or else you and I will become spoiled, pampered children.

Warren Wiersbe

Perseverance is more than endurance. It is endurance combined with absolute assurance and certainty that what we are looking for is going to happen.

Oswald Chambers

All rising to a great place is by a winding stair.

Francis Bacon

Only the man who follows the command of Jesus single-mindedly and unresistingly lets his yoke rest upon him, finds his burden easy, and under its gentle pressure receives the power to persevere in the right way.

Dietrich Bonhoeffer

Failure is one of life's most powerful teachers. How we handle our failures determines whether we're going to simply "get by" in life or "press on."

Beth Moore

By perseverance the snail reached the ark.

C. H. Spurgeon

As we find that it is not easy to persevere in this being "alone with God," we begin to realize that it is because we are not "wholly for God." God has a right to demand that He should have us completely for Himself.

Andrew Murray

When you persevere through a trial, God gives you a special measure of insight.

Charles Swindoll

POINTS OF EMPHASIS:
WRITE DOWN AT LEAST THREE THINGS THAT YOUR SON NEEDS TO HEAR FROM YOU ABOUT PATIENCE

18

Talk to Your Son About

Thinking Positively

Dear Son, You Can Control the Direction of Your Thoughts, and You Should.

Finally brothers, whatever is true, whatever is honorable, whatever is just, whatever is pure, whatever is lovely, whatever is commendable—if there is any moral excellence and if there is any praise—dwell on these things.

Philippians 4:8 HCSB

Do you pay careful attention to the quality of your thoughts? And are you teaching your son to do likewise? Hopefully so, because the quality of your thoughts will help determine the quality of your lives.

Ours is a society that focuses on—and often glamorizes—the negative aspects of life. So both you and your son will be bombarded with messages—some subtle and some overt—that encourage you to think cynically about your circumstances, your world, and your faith. But God has other plans for you and your youngster.

God promises that those who follow His Son, can experience joyful abundance (John 10:10). Consequently, Christianity and pessimism simply don't mix. So if you find that your thoughts are being hijacked by the negativity that seems to have invaded our troubled world, it's time to focus less on your challenges and more on God's blessings.

God intends for you and your family members to experience joy and abundance, not cynicism and negativity. So, today and every day hereafter, celebrate the life that God has given you by focusing your thoughts upon those things that are worthy of praise. And while you're at it, teach your son to do the same. When you do, you'll both discover that God's gifts are simply too glorious, and too numerous, to count.

Set your minds on what is above, not on what is on the earth.

Colossians 3:2 HCSB

Commit your works to the Lord, and your thoughts will be established.

Proverbs 16:3 NKJV

Brothers, don't be childish in your thinking, but be infants in evil and adult in your thinking.

1 Corinthians 14:20 HCSB

Guard your heart above all else, for it is the source of life.

Proverbs 4:23 HCSB

May the words of my mouth and the meditation of my heart be acceptable to You, Lord, my rock and my Redeemer.

Psalm 19:14 HCSB

MORE FROM GOD'S WORD ABOUT GOD'S BLESSINGS

You will show me the path of life; in Your presence is fullness of joy; at Your right hand are pleasures forevermore.

Psalm 16:11 NKJV

I will make them and the area around My hill a blessing: I will send down showers in their season—showers of blessing.

Ezekiel 34:26 HCSB

Obey My voice, and I will be your God, and you shall be my people. And walk in all the ways that I have commanded you, that it may be well with you.

Jeremiah 7:23 NKJV

The Lord bless you and keep you; the Lord make His face shine upon you, and be gracious to you.

Numbers 6:24-25 NKJV

Blessed is a man who endures trials, because when he passes the test he will receive the crown of life that He has promised to those who love Him.

James 1:12 HCSB

MORE FOOD FOR THOUGHT ABOUT GOD'S BLESSINGS

Preoccupy my thoughts with your praise beginning today.

Joni Eareckson Tada

Every major spiritual battle is in the mind.

Charles Stanley

Attitude is the mind's paintbrush; it can color any situation.

Barbara Johnson

Your thoughts are the determining factor as to whose mold you are conformed to. Control your thoughts and you control the direction of your life.

Charles Stanley

As we have by faith said no to sin, so we should by faith say yes to God and set our minds on things above, where Christ is seated in the heavenlies.

Vonette Bright

Beware of cut-and-dried theologies that reduce the ways of God to a manageable formula that keeps life safe. God often does the unexplainable just to keep us on our toes—and also on our knees.

Warren Wiersbe

I became aware of one very important concept I had missed before: my attitude—not my circumstances—was what was making me unhappy.

Vonette Bright

No more imperfect thoughts. No more sad memories. No more ignorance. My redeemed body will have a redeemed mind. Grant me a foretaste of that perfect mind as you mirror your thoughts in me today.

Joni Eareckson Tada

The things we think are the things that feed our souls. If we think on pure and lovely things, we shall grow pure and lovely like them; and the converse is equally true.

Hannah Whitall Smith

Points of Emphasis:
Write Down at least Three Things That Your Son Needs to Hear from You About God's Blessings

19

Talk to Your Son About

Financial Common Sense

DEAR SON, THE SOONER YOU LEARN TO MANAGE MONEY, THE BETTER. SO YOU MIGHT AS WELL LEARN NOW.

Good planning and hard work lead to prosperity,
but hasty shortcuts lead to poverty.

Proverbs 21:5 NLT

As a parent, you know, from firsthand experience, that the job of raising your son is an immense responsibility. And one of your parental duties is to teach your youngster how to manage money.

If you're serious about helping your son become a savvy spender and a serious saver, you must teach by example. After all, parental pronouncements are far easier to make than they are to live by. Yet your son will likely learn far more from your actions than from your words. So please remember that in matters of money, you are not just a role model; you are the role model. And as you begin to teach your child a few common-sense principles about spending and saving, remember that your actions will speak far more loudly than your words.

The world won't protect your son from the consequences of frivolous spending, and neither should you. So if he overspends, don't be too quick to bail him out of his troubles. As a parent, your job is not necessarily to protect your youngster from pain, but to ensure that he learns from the consequences of his actions.

Thankfully, the basic principles of money management aren't very hard to understand. These principles can be summed up in three simple steps: 1. Have a budget and live by it, spending less than you make; 2. Save and invest wisely; 3. Give God His fair share. These steps are so straightforward that even a young child can grasp them, so you need not have attended business school (or seminary) to teach powerful lessons about faith and finances. And that's good because your son needs your sound advice and your good example . . . but not necessarily in that order.

For I am the Lord, I do not change. Will a man rob God? Yet you have robbed Me! But you say, in what way have we robbed You? In tithes and offerings. You are cursed with a curse, for you have robbed Me, even this whole nation. Bring all the tithes into the storehouse, that there may be food in My house.

Malachi 3:6,8-10 NKJV

And my God shall supply all your need according to His riches in glory by Christ Jesus.

Philippians 4:19 NKJV

Based on the gift they have received, everyone should use it to serve others, as good managers of the varied grace of God.

1 Peter 4:10 HCSB

Your life should be free from the love of money. Be satisfied with what you have, for He Himself has said, I will never leave you or forsake you.

Hebrews 13:5 HCSB

MORE FOOD FOR THOUGHT ABOUT FINANCIAL COMMON SENSE

Jesus had much to say about money, . . . more than about almost any other subject.

Bill Bright

Sadly, family problems and even financial problems are seldom the real problem, but often the symptom of a weak or nonexistent value system.

Dave Ramsey

Here's a good recipe for managing your money: Never make a big financial decision without first talking it over with God.

Marie T. Freeman

There is nothing wrong with asking God's direction. But it is wrong to go our own way, then expect Him to bail us out.

Larry Burkett

If your outgo exceeds your income, then your upkeep will be your downfall.

John Maxwell

As faithful stewards of what we have, ought we not to give earnest thought to our staggering surplus?

Elisabeth Elliot

It is easy to determine the importance money plays in God's plan by the abundance of Scripture that relates to it—more than seven hundred verses directly refer to its use.

Larry Burkett

God meant that we adjust to the Gospel—not the other way around.

Vance Havner

POINTS OF EMPHASIS:
WRITE DOWN AT LEAST THREE THINGS THAT YOUR SON NEEDS TO HEAR FROM YOU ABOUT FINANCIAL COMMON SENSE

20

Talk to Your Son About

Addiction

Dear Son, Addictions Can Wreck Your Life, and the Easiest Way to Quit Is Never to Start.

You shall have no other gods before Me.

Exodus 20:3 NKJV

Your son inhabits a society that glamorizes the use of drugs, alcohol, cigarettes, and other addictive substances. Why? The answer can be summed up in one word: money. Simply put, addictive substances are big money makers, so suppliers (of both legal and illegal substances) work overtime to make certain that youngsters like your son sample their products. Since the suppliers need a steady stream of new customers because the old ones are dying off (fast), they engage in a no-holds-barred struggle to find new users—or more accurately, new abusers.

The dictionary defines *addiction* as "the compulsive need for a habit-forming substance; the condition of being habitually and compulsively occupied with something." That definition is accurate, but incomplete. For Christians, addiction has an additional meaning: it means compulsively worshipping something other than God.

Your son may already know youngsters who are full-blown addicts, but with God's help he can avoid that fate. To do so, he should learn that addictive substances are, in truth, spiritual and emotional poisons. And he must avoid the temptation to experiment with addictive substances. If he can do these things, he will spare himself a lifetime of headaches and heartaches.

Be sober! Be on the alert! Your adversary the Devil is prowling around like a roaring lion, looking for anyone he can devour.

1 Peter 5:8 HCSB

For we do not have a High Priest who cannot sympathize with our weaknesses, but was in all points tempted as we are, yet without sin. Let us therefore come boldly to the throne of grace, that we may obtain mercy and find grace to help in time of need.

Hebrews 4:15-16 NKJV

Jesus responded, "I assure you: Everyone who commits sin is a slave of sin."

John 8:34 HCSB

Death is the reward of an undisciplined life; your foolish decisions trap you in a dead end.

Proverbs 5:23 MSG

Yet in all these things we are more than conquerors through Him who loved us.

Romans 8:37 NKJV

MORE FOOD FOR THOUGHT ABOUT ABSTINENCE, MODERATION, VIRTUE, AND GOD

Virtue—even attempted virtue—brings light; indulgence brings fog.

C. S. Lewis

God is able to take mistakes, when they are committed to Him, and make of them something for our good and for His glory.

Ruth Bell Graham

To many, total abstinence is easier than perfect moderation.

St. Augustine

Nobody is good by accident. No man ever became holy by chance.

C. H. Spurgeon

When we face an impossible situation, all self-reliance and self-confidence must melt away; we must be totally dependent on Him for the resources.

Anne Graham Lotz

A live body is not one that never gets hurt, but one that can to some extent repair itself. In the same way a Christian is not a man who never goes wrong, but a man who is enabled to repent and pick himself up and begin over again after each stumble—because the Christ-life is inside him, repairing him all the time, enabling him to repeat (in some degree) the kind of voluntary death which Christ himself carried out.

C. S. Lewis

No matter how crazy or nutty your life has seemed, God can make something strong and good out of it. He can help you grow wide branches for others to use as shelter.

Barbara Johnson

A person may not be responsible for his last drink, but he certainly was for the first.

Billy Graham

Addiction is the most powerful psychic enemy of humanity's desire for God.

Gerald May

Points of Emphasis:
Write Down at least Three Things That Your Son Needs to Hear from You About Abstinence, Moderation, Virtue, and God

21

Talk to Your Son About

Being Healthy

Dear Son, Take Care of Your Body; It's the Only One You've Got.

Therefore, brothers, by the mercies of God,
I urge you to present your bodies as a living sacrifice,
holy and pleasing to God; this is your spiritual worship.

Romans 12:1 HCSB

In the Book of Romans, Paul encourages us to make our bodies "holy and pleasing to God." Paul adds that to do so is a "spiritual act of worship." For believers, the implication is clear: God intends that we take special care of the bodies He has given us. But it's tempting to do otherwise.

We live in a fast-food world where unhealthy choices are convenient, inexpensive, and tempting. And, we live in a digital world filled with modern conveniences that often rob us of the physical exercise needed to maintain healthy lifestyles. As a result, too many of us, adults and children alike, find ourselves glued to the television, with a snack in one hand and a clicker in the other. The results are as unfortunate as they are predictable.

As adults, each of us bears a personal responsibility for the general state of our own physical health. Certainly, various aspects of health are beyond our control: illness sometimes strikes even the healthiest people. But for most of us, physical health is a choice: it is the result of hundreds of small decisions that we make every day of our lives. If we make decisions that promote good health, our bodies respond. But if we fall into bad habits and undisciplined lifestyles, we suffer tragic consequences.

When our unhealthy habits lead to poor health, we find it all too easy to look beyond ourselves and assign blame. In fact, we live in a society where blame has become a national obsession: we blame cigarette manufacturers, restaurants, and food producers, to name only a few. But to blame others is to miss the point: We, and we alone, are responsible for the way that we treat our bodies. And the sooner that we accept that responsibility, the sooner we can assert control over our bodies and our lives.

Do you sincerely desire to improve your physical health? And do you wish to encourage your child to do likewise? If so, start by taking personal responsibility for the body that God has given you. Next, be sure to teach your son the common-sense lessons of sensible diet and regular exercise. Then, make a solemn pledge to yourself that you'll help your family make the choices that are necessary to enjoy longer, healthier, happier lives. No one can make those choices for you; you must make them for yourselves. And with God's help, you can . . . and you will.

Don't you know that you are God's sanctuary and that the Spirit of God lives in you?

1 Corinthians 3:16 HCSB

For it was You who created my inward parts; You knit me together in my mother's womb. I will praise You, because I have been remarkably and wonderfully made.

Psalm 139:13-14 HCSB

MORE FOOD FOR THOUGHT ABOUT BEING HEALTHY

God wants you to give Him your body. Some people do foolish things with their bodies. God wants your body as a holy sacrifice.

Warren Wiersbe

Stay busy. Get proper exercise. Eat the right foods. Don't spend time watching TV, lying in bed, or napping all day.

Truett Cathy

Exercise promotes the psychological benefits of looking and feeling healthy, and it reduces stress and stress-induced eating.

Dr. Richard Couey

Most people I know either love exercise and do it excessively, or they hate it and avoid it completely; yet consistent exercise is one of the keys to good health.

John Maxwell

The key to healthy eating is moderation and managing what you eat every day.

John Maxwell

You can't buy good health at the doctor's office—you've got to earn it for yourself.

Marie T. Freeman

People are funny. When they are young, they will spend their health to get wealth. Later, they will gladly pay all they have trying to get their health back.

John Maxwell

Ultimate healing and the glorification of the body are certainly among the blessings of Calvary for the believing Christian. Immediate healing is not guaranteed.

Warren Wiersbe

Exercise and physical fitness have a cause-and-effect relationship; fitness comes as a direct result of regular, sustained, and intense exercise.

John Maxwell

Points of Emphasis:
Write Down at least Three Things That Your Son Needs to Hear from You About Health

22

Talk to Your Son About
Materialism

Dear Son, Material Possessions Aren't as Important as You Think.

No one can serve two masters.
The person will hate one master and love the other,
or will follow one master and refuse to follow the other.
You cannot serve both God and worldly riches.

Matthew 6:24 NCV

Your son inhabits a world in which material possessions are, at times, glamorized and, at other times, almost worshipped. The media often glorifies material possessions above all else, but God most certainly does not. And it's up to you, as a responsible parent, to make certain that your child understands that materialism is a spiritual trap, a trap that should be avoided at all costs.

Martin Luther observed, "Many things I have tried to grasp and have lost. That which I have placed in God's hands I still have." His words apply to all of us. Our earthly riches are transitory; our spiritual riches, on the other hand, are everlasting.

If you find yourself wrapped up in the concerns of the material world, you can be sure that your family members are wrapped up in it, too. So how much stuff is too much stuff? It's a tough question for many of us, yet the answer is straightforward: If our possessions begin to interfere with our desire to know and serve God, then we own too many possessions, period.

On the grand stage of a well-lived life, material possessions should play a rather small role. Of course, we all need the basic necessities of life, but once we meet those needs for ourselves and for our families, the piling up of possessions creates more problems than it solves. Our real riches, of course, are not of this world. We are never really rich until we are rich in spirit.

So, if you or your family members find yourselves wrapped up in the concerns of the material world, it's time to reorder your priorities. And, it's time to begin storing up riches that will endure throughout eternity—the spiritual kind.

And He told them, "Watch out and be on guard against all greed, because one's life is not in the abundance of his possessions."

Luke 12:15 HCSB

For what does it benefit a man to gain the whole world yet lose his life? What can a man give in exchange for his life?

Mark 8:36-37 HCSB

Don't collect for yourselves treasures on earth, where moth and rust destroy and where thieves break in and steal. But collect for yourselves treasures in heaven, where neither moth nor rust destroys, and where thieves don't break in and steal. For where your treasure is, there your heart will be also.

Matthew 6:19-21 HCSB

Anyone trusting in his riches will fall, but the righteous will flourish like foliage.

Proverbs 11:28 HCSB

More from God's Word About Worldliness

Let no one deceive himself. If anyone among you seems to be wise in this age, let him become a fool that he may become wise. For the wisdom of this world is foolishness with God. For it is written, "He catches the wise in their own craftiness."

1 Corinthians 3:18–19 NKJV

Do not love the world or the things in the world. If you love the world, the love of the Father is not in you.

1 John 2:15 NCV

For whatever is born of God overcomes the world. And this is the victory that has overcome the world—our faith.

1 John 5:4 NKJV

If you lived on the world's terms, the world would love you as one of its own. But since I picked you to live on God's terms and no longer on the world's terms, the world is going to hate you.

John 15:19 MSG

MORE FOOD FOR THOUGHT ABOUT WORLDLINESS

If you want to be truly happy, you won't find it on an endless quest for more stuff. You'll find it in receiving God's generosity and in passing that generosity along.

Bill Hybels

The Scriptures also reveal warning that if we are consumed with greed, not only do we disobey God, but we will miss the opportunity to allow Him to use us as instruments for others.

Charles Stanley

We own too many things that aren't worth owning.

Marie T. Freeman

Here's a simple test: If you can see it, it's not going to last. The things that last are the things you cannot see.

Dennis Swanberg

Why is love of gold more potent than love of souls?

Lottie Moon

The cross is laid on every Christian. It begins with the call to abandon the attachments of this world.

Dietrich Bonhoeffer

A society that pursues pleasure runs the risk of raising expectations ever higher, so that true contentment always lies tantalizingly out of reach.

Philip Yancey and Paul Brand

Getting a little greedy? Pray without seizing.

Anonymous

There is absolutely no evidence that complexity and materialism lead to happiness. On the contrary, there is plenty of evidence that simplicity and spirituality lead to joy, a blessedness that is better than happiness.

Dennis Swanberg

POINTS OF EMPHASIS:
WRITE DOWN AT LEAST THREE THINGS THAT YOUR SON NEEDS TO HEAR FROM YOU ABOUT WORLDLINESS

23

Talk to Your Son About

Temptation

DEAR SON, THE WORLD IS FILLED WITH TEMPTATIONS THAT CAN WRECK YOUR LIFE; BEHAVE ACCORDINGLY.

My son, if sinners entice you, don't be persuaded.

Proverbs 1:10 HCSB

Because our world is filled with temptations, your son will encounter them at every turn. The devil, it seems, is working overtime these days, causing heartache in more places and in more ways than ever before. So your youngster must remain vigilant. How? By avoiding those places where Satan can most easily tempt him and by arming himself with God's Holy Word.

After fasting forty days and nights in the desert, Jesus Himself was tempted by Satan. Christ used Scripture to rebuke the devil (Matthew 4:1-11). We must do likewise. The Holy Bible provides us with a perfect blueprint for righteous living. If we consult that blueprint each day and follow its instructions carefully, we build our lives according to God's plan. And when we do, we are secure.

Your youngster lives in a society that encourages him to "try" any number of things that are dangerous to his spiritual, mental, or physical health. It's a world brimming with traps and temptations designed to corrupt his character, ruin his health, sabotage his relationships, and derail his future. Your job, as a thoughtful parent, is to warn your son of these dangers . . . and to keep warning him.

No temptation has overtaken you except what is common to humanity. God is faithful and He will not allow you to be tempted beyond what you are able, but with the temptation He will also provide a way of escape, so that you are able to bear it.

1 Corinthians 10:13 HCSB

Put on the full armor of God so that you can stand against the tactics of the Devil.

Ephesians 6:11 HCSB

Stay awake and pray, so that you won't enter into temptation. The spirit is willing, but the flesh is weak.

Matthew 26:41 HCSB

The Spirit's law of life in Christ Jesus has set you free from the law of sin and of death.

Romans 8:2 HCSB

MORE FROM GOD'S WORD ABOUT GUARDING AGAINST EVIL

Above all else, guard your heart, for it affects everything you do.

Proverbs 4:23 NLT

The peace of God, which surpasses all understanding, will guard your hearts and minds through Christ Jesus.

Philippians 4:7 NKJV

Don't copy the behavior and customs of this world, but let God transform you into a new person by changing the way you think. Then you will know what God wants you to do, and you will know how good and pleasing and perfect his will really is.

Romans 12:2 NLT

Do not fret because of evildoers; don't envy the wicked.

Proverbs 24:19 NLT

Therefore, submit to God. But resist the Devil, and he will flee from you. Draw near to God, and He will draw near to you. Cleanse your hands, sinners, and purify your hearts, double-minded people!

James 4:7-8 HCSB

More Food for Thought About Guarding Against Evil

Don't say you have a chaste mind if you have an unchaste eye, because the unchaste eye is the messenger of an unchaste heart.

St. Augustine

In the worst temptations nothing can help us but faith that God's Son has put on flesh, sits at the right hand of the Father, and prays for us. There is no mightier comfort.

Martin Luther

Most Christians do not know or fully realize that the adversary of our lives is Satan and that his main tool is our flesh, our old nature.

Bill Bright

A man who gives in to temptation after five minutes simply does not know what it would have been like an hour later.

C. S. Lewis

Take a really honest look at yourself. Have any old sins begun to take control again? This would be a wonderful time to allow Him to bring fresh order out of longstanding chaos.

Charles Swindoll

Since you are tempted without ceasing, pray without ceasing.

C. H. Spurgeon

Many times the greatest temptations confront us when we are in the center of the will of God, because being there has offset and frustrated Satans' methods of attack.

Franklin Graham

The Bible teaches us in times of temptation there is one command: Flee! Get away from it, for every struggle against lust using only one's own strength is doomed to failure.

Dietrich Bonhoeffer

It is easier to stay out of temptation than to get out of it.

Rick Warren

Points of Emphasis:
Write Down at least Three Things That Your Son Needs to Hear from You About Guarding Against Evil

24

Talk to Your Son About
Peer Pressure

DEAR SON, SINCE YOU'LL INEVITABLY BECOME MORE LIKE YOUR FRIENDS, CHOOSE YOUR FRIENDS WISELY.

Do not be deceived: "Bad company corrupts good morals."

1 Corinthians 15:33 HCSB

Peer pressure can be a good thing or a bad thing for your son, depending upon his peers. If his peers encourage him to make integrity a habit—if they encourage him to follow God's will and to obey God's commandments—your son will experience positive peer pressure, and that's good.

But, if your youngster becomes involved with people who encourage him to do foolish things, he'll face a different kind of peer pressure. If your son feels pressured to do things or to say things that lead him away from God, he's aiming straight for trouble.

As you talk to your child about the differences between positive and negative peer pressure, here are a few things to emphasize:

1. Peer pressure exists, and your son will experience it.
2. If your son's friends encourage him to honor God and become a better person, peer pressure can be a good thing.
3. If your son's friends encourage him to misbehave or underachieve, that sort of peer pressure is destructive.
4. When peer pressure turns negative, it's up to your son to start finding new friends. Today.

To sum it up, your boy has a choice: he can choose to please God first, or he can fall prey to negative peer pressure. The choice is his—and so are the consequences.

He who walks with wise men will be wise, but the companion of fools will be destroyed.

Proverbs 13:20 NKJV

For am I now trying to win the favor of people, or God? Or am I striving to please people? If I were still trying to please people, I would not be a slave of Christ.

Galatians 1:10 HCSB

Stay away from a foolish man; you will gain no knowledge from his speech.

Proverbs 14:7 HCSB

My son, if sinners entice you, don't be persuaded.

Proverbs 1:10 HCSB

Blessed is the man who walks not in the counsel of the ungodly, nor stands in the path of sinners, nor sits in the seat of the scornful; but his delight is in the law of the Lord, and in His law he meditates day and night.

Psalm 1:1-2 NKJV

MORE FOOD FOR THOUGHT ABOUT PEER PRESSURE

Do you want to be wise? Choose wise friends.

Charles Swindoll

Comparison is the root of all feelings of inferiority.

James Dobson

You must never sacrifice your relationship with God for the sake of a relationship with another person.

Charles Stanley

It is impossible to please God doing things motivated by and produced by the flesh.

Bill Bright

It is comfortable to know that we are responsible to God and not to man. It is a small matter to be judged of man's judgement.

Lottie Moon

True friends will always lift you higher and challenge you to walk in a manner pleasing to our Lord.

Lisa Bevere

You should forget about trying to be popular with everybody and start trying to be popular with God Almighty.

Sam Jones

If you choose to awaken a passion for God, you will have to choose your friends wisely.

Lisa Bevere

People who constantly, and fervently, seek the approval of others live with an identity crisis. They don't know who they are, and they are defined by what others think of them.

Charles Stanley

Points of Emphasis:
Write Down at least Three Things That Your Son Needs to Hear from You About Peer Pressure

25

Talk to Your Son About
Avoiding Needless Risks

Dear Son, Some Risks Are Worth It, and Some Risks Aren't; It's Up to You to Figure Out the Difference.

Enthusiasm without knowledge is not good.
If you act too quickly, you might make a mistake.
Proverbs 19:2 NCV

Is your son, at times, just a bit too impulsive for his own good? Does he occasionally leap before he looks? Does he react first and think about his reaction second? And, as a result, does he occasionally take risks that he should not take? If so, God wants to have a little chat with him.

God's Word is clear: as believers, we are called to lead lives of discipline, diligence, moderation, and maturity. But the world often tempts us to behave otherwise. Everywhere we turn, or so it seems, we are faced with powerful temptations to behave in undisciplined, ungodly ways.

God's Word instructs us to be disciplined in our thoughts and our actions; God's Word warns us against the dangers of impulsive behavior. God's Word teaches us that "anger" is only one letter away from "danger." And, as believers in a just God who means what He says, your son should act—and react—accordingly.

The wise inherit honor, but fools are put to shame!

Proverbs 3:35 NLT

Grow a wise heart—you'll do yourself a favor; keep a clear head—you'll find a good life.

Proverbs 19:8 MSG

The one who walks with the wise will become wise, but a companion of fools will suffer harm.

Proverbs 13:20 HCSB

But if any of you needs wisdom, you should ask God for it. He is generous and enjoys giving to all people, so he will give you wisdom.

James 1:5 NCV

Those who are wise will shine as bright as the sky, and those who turn many to righteousness will shine like stars forever.

Daniel 12:3 NLT

MORE FOOD FOR THOUGHT ABOUT RISK

The really committed leave the safety of the harbor, accept the risk of the open seas of faith, and set their compasses for the place of total devotion to God and whatever life adventures He plans for them.

Bill Hybels

You never know how much you really believe anything until its truth or falsehood becomes a matter of life and death to you. It is easy to say you believe a rope to be strong and sound as long as you are merely using it to cord a box. But suppose you had to hang by that rope over a precipice. Wouldn't you then first discover how much you really trusted it? Only a real risk tests the reality of a belief.

C. S. Lewis

When I am secure in Christ, I can afford to take a risk in my life. Only the insecure cannot afford to risk failure. The secure can be honest about themselves; they can admit failure; they are able to seek help and try again. They can change.

John Maxwell

Two signposts of faith: "Slow Down" and "Wait Here."

Charles Stanley

There comes a time when we simply have to face the challenges in our lives and stop backing down.

John Eldredge

Risk must be taken because the greatest hazard in life is to risk nothing.

John Maxwell

If you want to walk on water . . . you've got to get out of the boat!

Anonymous

We live in a world where you can afford to fail and try again.

Dennis Swanberg

Points of Emphasis:
Write Down at least Three Things That Your Son Needs to Hear from You About Risk

26

Talk to Your Son About

Prayer

DEAR SON, PRAYER IS MORE POWERFUL THAN YOU THINK, SO IF YOU NEED SOMETHING, ASK GOD.

So I say to you, keep asking, and it will be given to you.
Keep searching, and you will find.
Keep knocking, and the door will be opened to you.

Luke 11:9 HCSB

Genuine, heartfelt prayer produces powerful changes in us and in our world. When we lift our hearts to God, we open ourselves to a never-ending source of divine wisdom and infinite love. So as a Christian parent, you must make certain that your child understands the power of prayer and the need for prayer. And the best way to do so, of course, is by example.

Is prayer an integral part of your family's life, or is it a hit-or-miss habit? Do you "pray without ceasing," or is your prayer life an afterthought? Do you regularly honor God in the solitude of the early morning darkness, or do you bow your head only when others are watching?

The quality of your son's spiritual life will be in direct proportion to the quality of his prayer life. Prayer changes things, and it will change him. So when you can tell he's turning things over in his mind, encourage him to turn them over to God in prayer. And while you're at it, don't limit your family's prayers to meals or to bedtime. Make sure that your family is constantly praying about things great and small because God is listening, and He wants to hear from you now.

Do not worry about anything, but pray and ask God for everything you need, always giving thanks.

Philippians 4:6 NCV

You do not have, because you do not ask God.

James 4:2 NIV

Verily, verily, I say unto you, He that believeth on me, the works that I do shall he do also; and greater works than these shall he do; because I go unto my Father. And whatsoever ye shall ask in my name, that will I do, that the Father may be glorified in the Son. If ye shall ask any thing in my name, I will do it.

John 14:12-14 KJV

You did not choose me, but I chose you and appointed you to go and bear fruit—fruit that will last. Then the Father will give you whatever you ask in my name.

John 15:16 NIV

Let us hold fast the confession of our hope without wavering, for He who promised is faithful.

Hebrews 10:23 NASB

MORE FROM GOD'S WORD ABOUT PRAYER

The intense prayer of the righteous is very powerful.

James 5:16 HCSB

Let the words of my mouth and the meditation of my heart be acceptable in Your sight, O Lord, my strength and my Redeemer.

Psalm 19:14 NKJV

Yet He often withdrew to deserted places and prayed.

Luke 5:16 HCSB

Don't worry about anything, but in everything, through prayer and petition with thanksgiving, let your requests be made known to God.

Philippians 4:6 HCSB

Rejoice in hope; be patient in affliction; be persistent in prayer.

Romans 12:12 HCSB

MORE FOOD FOR THOUGHT ABOUT PRAYER

Some people think God does not like to be troubled with our constant asking. But, the way to trouble God is not to come at all.

D. L. Moody

Notice that we must ask. And we will sometimes struggle to hear and struggle with what we hear. But personally, it's worth it. I'm after the path of life—and he alone knows it.

John Eldredge

God's help is always available, but it is only given to those who seek it.

Max Lucado

Don't be afraid to ask your heavenly Father for anything you need. Indeed, nothing is too small for God's attention or too great for his power.

Dennis Swanberg

God will help us become the people we are meant to be, if only we will ask Him.

Hannah Whitall Smith

True prayer is measured by weight, not by length. A single groan before God may have more fullness of prayer in it than a fine oration of great length.

C. H. Spurgeon

All we have to do is to acknowledge our need, move from self-sufficiency to dependence, and ask God to become our hiding place.

Bill Hybels

If you want more from life, ask more from God.

Criswell Freeman

We honor God by asking for great things when they are a part of His promise. We dishonor Him and cheat ourselves when we ask for molehills where He has promised mountains.

Vance Havner

POINTS OF EMPHASIS:
WRITE DOWN AT LEAST THREE THINGS THAT YOUR SON NEEDS TO HEAR FROM YOU ABOUT PRAYER

27

Talk to Your Son About

Maintaining Proper Perspective

**DEAR SON,
AS YOU GROW OLDER,
THINGS WILL HAPPEN
THAT YOU SIMPLY CANNOT
UNDERSTAND UNLESS YOU
REMEMBER THAT GOD HAS
AN ETERNAL PERSPECTIVE.**

Set your minds on what is above, not on what is on the earth.

Colossians 3:2 HCSB

For parents and kids alike, life is busy and complicated. Amid the rush and crush of the daily grind, it is easy to lose perspective . . . easy, but wrong. When our world seems to be spinning out of control, we can regain perspective by slowing down long enough to put things in proper perspective. But slowing down isn't always easy, especially for young people. So your son may, on occasion, become convinced (wrongly) that today's problems are both permanent and catastrophic. And if he starts making mountains out of molehills, it's up to you, as a thoughtful parent, to teach him how to regain perspective.

When you have a problem that seems overwhelming, do you carve out quiet moments to think about God's promises and what those promises mean in the grand scope of eternity? Are you wise enough to offer thanksgiving and praise to your Creator, in good times and bad? And do you encourage your son to do the same? If so, your child will be blessed by your instruction and your example.

The familiar words of Psalm 46:10 remind us to "Be still, and know that I am God" (NKJV). When we do so, we encounter the awesome presence of our Heavenly Father. But, when we ignore the presence of our Creator, we rob ourselves of His perspective, His peace, and His joy.

So today and every day, make time to be still before the Creator, and encourage your son to do likewise. Then, both of you can face life's inevitable setbacks—all of which, by the way, are temporary setbacks—with the wisdom and power that only God can provide.

Now if any of you lacks wisdom, he should ask God, who gives to all generously and without criticizing, and it will be given to him.

James 1:5 HCSB

For now we see in a mirror, dimly, but then face to face. Now I know in part, but then I shall know just as I also am known.

1 Corinthians 13:12 NKJV

Let no one deceive himself. If anyone among you seems to be wise in this age, let him become a fool that he may become wise. For the wisdom of this world is foolishness with God. For it is written, "He catches the wise in their own craftiness."

1 Corinthians 3:18-19 NKJV

So teach us to number our days, that we may gain a heart of wisdom.

Psalm 90:12 NKJV

MORE FROM GOD'S WORD ABOUT WISDOM

Don't abandon wisdom, and she will watch over you; love her, and she will guard you.

Proverbs 4:6 HCSB

Acquire wisdom—how much better it is than gold! And acquire understanding—it is preferable to silver.

Proverbs 16:16 HCSB

The one who acquires good sense loves himself; one who safeguards understanding finds success.

Proverbs 19:8 HCSB

Pay careful attention, then, to how you walk—not as unwise people but as wise.

Ephesians 5:15 HCSB

Who is wise and understanding among you? Let him show by good conduct that his works are done in the meekness of wisdom.

James 3:13 NKJV

MORE FOOD FOR THOUGHT ABOUT WISDOM

Life: the time God gives you to determine how you spend eternity.

Anonymous

All that is not eternal is eternally out of date.

C. S. Lewis

Salvation involves so much more than knowing facts about Jesus Christ, or even having special feelings toward Jesus Christ. Salvation comes to us when, by an act of will, we receive Christ as our Savior and Lord.

Warren Wiersbe

We are always trying to "find ourselves" when that is exactly what we need to lose.

Vance Havner

Going to church does not make you a Christian anymore than going to McDonald's makes you a hamburger.

Anonymous

I now know the power of the risen Lord! He lives! The dawn of Easter has broken in my own soul! My night is gone!

Mrs. Charles E. Cowman

The crucial question for each of us is this: What do you think of Jesus, and do you yet have a personal acquaintance with Him?

Hannah Whitall Smith

God is God. He knows what he is doing. When you can't trace his hand, trust his heart.

Max Lucado

As you and I lay up for ourselves living, lasting treasures in Heaven, we come to the awesome conclusion that we ourselves are His treasure!

Anne Graham Lotz

POINTS OF EMPHASIS:
WRITE DOWN AT LEAST THREE THINGS THAT YOUR SON NEEDS TO HEAR FROM YOU ABOUT WISDOM

28

Talk to Your Son About

Overcoming Tough Times

Dear Son, The Fact That You Encounter Tough Times Is Not Nearly as Important as the Way You Choose to Deal with Them.

God blesses the people who patiently endure testing. Afterward they will receive the crown of life that God has promised to those who love him.

James 1:12 NLT

Every human life (including your son's) is a tapestry of events: some grand, some not-so-grand, and some downright disheartening. When your child reaches the mountaintops of life, he'll find that praising God is easy. But, when the storm clouds form overhead and he finds himself in the dark valleys of life, his faith will be stretched, sometimes to the breaking point.

As Christians, we can be comforted: Wherever we find ourselves, whether at the top of the mountain or the depths of the valley, God is there, and because He cares for us, we can live courageously.

The Bible promises this: tough times are temporary but God's love is not—God's love lasts forever. Psalm 147 promises, "He heals the brokenhearted and binds up their wounds" (v. 3, HCSB), but Psalm 147 doesn't say that He heals them instantly. Usually, it takes time (and effort) to fix things.

So your son should learn that when he faces tough times, he should face them with God by his side. Your son should understand that when he encounters setbacks—and he will—he should always ask for God's help. And your son should learn to be patient. God will work things out, just as He has promised, but He will do it in His own way and in His own time.

When you are in distress and all these things have happened to you, you will return to the Lord your God in later days and obey Him. He will not leave you, destroy you, or forget the covenant with your fathers that He swore to them by oath, because the Lord your God is a compassionate God.

Deuteronomy 4:30-31 HCSB

Whatever has been born of God conquers the world. This is the victory that has conquered the world: our faith.

1 John 5:4 HCSB

Dear friends, when the fiery ordeal arises among you to test you, don't be surprised by it, as if something unusual were happening to you. Instead, as you share in the sufferings of the Messiah rejoice, so that you may also rejoice with great joy at the revelation of His glory.

1 Peter 4:12-13 HCSB

We are pressured in every way but not crushed; we are perplexed but not in despair.

2 Corinthians 4:8 HCSB

I called to the Lord in my distress; I called to my God. From His temple He heard my voice.

2 Samuel 22:7 HCSB

More Food for Thought About Adversity

The sermon of your life in tough times ministers to people more powerfully than the most eloquent speaker.

Bill Bright

Sometimes we get tired of the burdens of life, but we know that Jesus Christ will meet us at the end of life's journey. And, that makes all the difference.

Billy Graham

God allows us to experience the low points of life in order to teach us lessons that we could learn in no other way.

C. S. Lewis

Life will be made or broken at the place where we meet and deal with obstacles.

E. Stanley Jones

It is true of every stinging experience of our lives: Jesus, and Jesus alone, can rescue us.

Franklin Graham

People who inspire others are those who see invisible bridges at the end of dead-end streets.

Charles Swindoll

Our loving God uses difficulty in our lives to burn away the sin of self and build faith and spiritual power.

Bill Bright

Adversity is always unexpected and unwelcomed. It is an intruder and a thief, and yet in the hands of God, adversity becomes the means through which His supernatural power is demonstrated.

Charles Swindoll

We can stand affliction better than we can stand prosperity, for in prosperity we forget God.

D. L. Moody

POINTS OF EMPHASIS:
WRITE DOWN AT LEAST THREE THINGS THAT YOUR SON NEEDS TO HEAR FROM YOU ABOUT ADVERSITY

29

Talk to Your Son About

Hope

DEAR SON, NEVER STOP BELIEVING IN A BRIGHTER FUTURE.

There is surely a future hope for you,
and your hope will not be cut off.

Proverbs 23:18 NIV

The hope that the world offers is fleeting and imperfect. The hope that God offers is unchanging, unshakable, and unending. It is no wonder, then, that when we seek security from worldly sources, our hopes are often dashed. Thankfully, God has no such record of failure.

Because we are saved by a risen Christ, we can have hope for the future, no matter how troublesome our present circumstances may seem. After all, God has promised that we are His throughout eternity. And, He has told us that we must place our hopes in Him.

All of us, parents and children alike, will face disappointments and failures while we are here on earth, but these are only temporary defeats. Of course, this world can be a place of trials and tribulations, but when we place our trust in the Giver of all things good, we are secure. God has promised us peace, joy, and eternal life. And God keeps His promises today, tomorrow, and forever.

Are you willing to place your future in the hands of a loving and all-knowing God? Will you face today's challenges with optimism and hope? Will you encourage your son to do the same? Hopefully, you can answer these questions with a resounding yes. After all, God created you and your child for very important purposes: His purposes. And you both still have important work to do: His work.

So today, as you live in the present and look to the future, remember that God has a plan for you and your son. And it's up to both of you to act—and to believe—accordingly.

Be of good courage, and he shall strengthen your heart, all ye that hope in the LORD.

Psalm 31:24 KJV

Be joyful in hope, patient in affliction, faithful in prayer.

Romans 12:12 NIV

The Lord is good to those whose hope is in him, to the one who seeks him; it is good to wait quietly for the salvation of the Lord.

Lamentations 3:25-26 NIV

May the God of hope fill you with all joy and peace as you trust in him, so that you may overflow with hope by the power of the Holy Spirit.

Romans 15:13 NIV

MORE FOOD FOR THOUGHT ABOUT THE FUTURE AND HOPE

I wish I could make it all new again; I can't. But God can. "He restores my soul," wrote the shepherd. God doesn't reform; he restores. He doesn't camouflage the old; he restores the new. The Master Builder will pull out the original plan and restore it. He will restore the vigor, he will restore the energy. He will restore the hope. He will restore the soul.

Max Lucado

Faith looks back and draws courage; hope looks ahead and keeps desire alive.

John Eldredge

Hope is nothing more than the expectation of those things which faith has believed to be truly promised by God.

John Calvin

The hope we have in Jesus is the anchor for the soul—something sure and steadfast, preventing drifting or giving way, lowered to the depth of God's love.

Franklin Graham

Oh, remember this: There is never a time when we may not hope in God. Whatever our necessities, however great our difficulties, and though to all appearance help is impossible, yet our business is to hope in God, and it will be found that it is not in vain.

George Mueller

The Christian believes in a fabulous future.

Billy Graham

Take courage. We walk in the wilderness today and in the Promised Land tomorrow.

D. L. Moody

It may be that the day of judgment will dawn tomorrow; in that case, we shall gladly stop working for a better tomorrow. But not before.

Dietrich Bonhoeffer

Joy comes from knowing God loves me and knows who I am and where I'm going . . . that my future is secure as I rest in Him.

James Dobson

Points of Emphasis:
Write Down at least Three Things That Your Son Needs to Hear from You About the Future and Hope

30

Talk to Your Son About

Eternal Life

DEAR SON, JESUS OFFERS THE GIFT ETERNAL LIFE, AND THE REST IS UP TO YOU.

"I assure you: Anyone who hears My word and believes Him who sent Me has eternal life and will not come under judgment, but has passed from death to life."

John 5:24–25 HCSB

Eternal life is not an event that begins when we die. Eternal life begins when we invite Jesus into our hearts. The moment we allow Jesus to reign over our hearts, we've already begun our eternal journeys.

As a thoughtful Christian parent, it's important to remind your child that God's plans are not limited to the ups and downs of everyday life. In fact, the ups and downs of the daily grind are, quite often, impossible for us to understand. As mere mortals, our understanding of the present and our visions for the future—like our lives here on earth—are limited. God's vision is not burdened by such limitations: His plans extend throughout all eternity. And we must trust Him even when we cannot understand the particular details of His plan.

So let us praise the Creator for His priceless gift, and let us share the Good News with all who cross our paths. We return our Father's love by accepting His grace and by sharing His message and His love. When we do, we are blessed here on earth and throughout all eternity.

And this is the testimony: God has given us eternal life, and this life is in His Son. The one who has the Son has life. The one who doesn't have the Son of God does not have life. I have written these things to you who believe in the name of the Son of God, so that you may know that you have eternal life.

1 John 5:11-13 HCSB

We do not want you to be uninformed, brothers, concerning those who are asleep, so that you will not grieve like the rest, who have no hope. Since we believe that Jesus died and rose again, in the same way God will bring with Him those who have fallen asleep through Jesus.

1 Thessalonians 4:13-14 HCSB

Jesus said to her, "I am the resurrection and the life. The one who believes in Me, even if he dies, will live. Everyone who lives and believes in Me will never die—ever. Do you believe this?"

John 11:25-26 HCSB

Pursue righteousness, godliness, faith, love, endurance, and gentleness. Fight the good fight for the faith; take hold of eternal life, to which you were called and have made a good confession before many witnesses.

1 Timothy 6:11-12 HCSB

MORE FOOD FOR THOUGHT ABOUT ETERNAL LIFE

And because we know Christ is alive, we have hope for the present and hope for life beyond the grave.

Billy Graham

Someday you will read in the papers that Moody is dead. Don't you believe a word of it. At that moment I shall be more alive than I am now. I was born of the flesh in 1837, I was born of the spirit in 1855. That which is born of the flesh may die. That which is born of the Spirit shall live forever.

D. L. Moody

Once a man is united to God, how could he not live forever? Once a man is separated from God, what can he do but wither and die?

C. S. Lewis

Let us see the victorious Jesus, the conqueror of the tomb, the one who defied death. And let us be reminded that we, too, will be granted the same victory.

Max Lucado

Slowly and surely, we learn the great secret of life, which is to know God.

Oswald Chambers

The damage done to us on this earth will never find its way into that safe city. We can relax, we can rest, and though some of us can hardly imagine it, we can prepare to feel safe and secure for all of eternity.

Bill Hybels

God did not spring forth from eternity; He brought forth eternity.

C. H. Spurgeon

God's salvation comes as gift; it is eternal, and it is a continuum, meaning it starts when I receive the gift in faith and is never-ending.

Franklin Graham

Turn your life over to Christ today, and your life will never be the same.

Billy Graham

Points of Emphasis:
Write Down at least Three Things That Your Son Needs to Hear from You About Eternal Life

More Ideas from Mom and Dad

On the following pages, jot down any more lessons, stories, or insights that you wish to share with your son.